WE WERE THERE
ON THE
CHISHOLM TRAIL

WE WERE THERE
ON THE
Chisholm Trail

By ROSS McLAURY TAYLOR

Historical Consultant: STANLEY VESTAL
Illustrated by CHARLES BANKS WILSON

GROSSET & DUNLAP *Publishers*
NEW YORK

© ROSS MCLAURY TAYLOR 1957

*This book
is affectionately dedicated
to*
JOHN FRANCIS TAYLOR
and
LEIGH PAULETTE UNDERWOOD
*Two lovely little people
with whom anyone would like
to travel a trail*

Contents

Illustrations

[*ix*]

WE WERE THERE
ON THE
CHISHOLM TRAIL

Lance and his father heard the mutter of thunder

CHAPTER ONE

Down the Valley to the Trail

EVEN through the choking dust cloud raised by the trampling of eleven hundred shaggy long-horns, Lance Calhoun could feel the change in the weather. Since early morning, the wind had blown from the north across the wide valley below the plateau, dry and cold. Now, just before twilight, huge black clouds pushed up from the Gulf of Mexico to the south, and with them came a new breeze that was light and warm and damp.

The steers felt it and quieted for a moment, snuffing. Lance rode his paint gelding around the spreading herd and up the slope of the valley to join his father.

For a moment, they halted their horses and looked back over the V-shaped valley. Far down at the mouth of the valley, they could see the long line of high-piled stickery brush and mesquite that made a fence to hold the trail herd. Without that fence, Lance thought, those steers would run back to the brush country and go wild. Six months' work would be lost. They were a shaggy lot, with horns spreading four, five, even six feet, and they could run like deer.

"Not a bad steer in the herd, Lance!" His father slapped him on the shoulder. "Prime beef! In the morning, we take them up the Chisholm Trail to Mr. McCoy in Abilene."

Lance watched through the twilight haze, made deeper by bluebonnets growing everywhere on the slopes of the valley. He listened to the sounds of the quieting herd and watched the wind writing clouds on the evening sky.

For as long as he could remember, he had always wanted to be a rancher like his father. Now, at last, he was fourteen. He had his own three horses, a new saddle, a carbine in the saddle boot, a bedroll and tarpaulin of his own—and he was headed up the Chisholm Trail!

As they rode along the valley toward the edge of the plateau, Lance and his father heard the mutter of thunder. Towering clouds boiled into the sky, and darkness blotted out the vast, low-sprawling ranch house and bunkhouse and stables and corrals. In the flickering lightning, Lance could see his mother, her skirts swirling in the lifting wind. Beside her stood the smaller figure of Cousin Lou Ann. His "almost cousin," he thought, as he remembered that Lou Ann's mother had been his mother's closest friend a long time ago. Tomorrow, Lou Ann would go with them on the cattle drive. When they reached Abilene, she'd go back home to St. Louis, she and Tina, the little Spanish Barb mare she rode.

Lance and his father could hear the punchers coming up behind them as they rode for the corral and the stables. A giant wind blew fiercely across the ranch yard, and the smell of fresh rain was perfume in the air. Thunder crashed like boulders down a mountainside as father and son rubbed down their horses and fed them. Outside the kitchen at the ranch house, Lance could hear Juan Santiago hammering on the old ship's bell.

"Cookie! Cookie! Come and get it! Come and get it!"

As they ran through the misty rain to the

[5]

house, Lance saw the big canvas-covered chuck wagon, already loaded with a part of their food and sleeping gear. Next to it stood the light spring-bed wagon Lou Ann would drive, its cover flapping in the wind, waiting to be hitched in the morning. Under the shelter of the veranda, running the length of the old stone ranch house, Sarah Calhoun and Lou Ann waited with towels for Lance and his father.

"Oh, Bruce Calhoun, you're wet and dripping!" Lance's mother scrubbed at his father's face. "This rain will ruin everything."

"And you're wet, too, Lance!" Lou Ann mimicked his mother.

"This is just a March storm, Sarah—the end of the winter and the beginning of spring," Colonel Calhoun said. "It will stop before morning."

Lightning made Lou Ann's copper-red hair flame in the blaze of light. She had changed, Lance thought. She wasn't the sickly little girl who had come down the big river from St. Louis and way out to south Texas a year and a half ago. Now she was almost grown up, his own age, and standing so proud.

After supper at the long table in the big room

with the fire crackling and popping a merry tune, Lance's father pushed back in his chair. For a moment, his fingers traced his cavalryman's mustaches, and his gray eyes flashed.

"I'm worried," said Mrs. Calhoun, shaking her head. "This weather!"

"This will blow over tonight, Sarah," Colonel Calhoun reassured her again. "It's a spring storm from the Gulf of Mexico. Bluebonnets are out. It's pushing the season, but I want to be the first up the Trail. Lou Ann will be all right. There'll be ten of us to look after her."

He looked at Lance's twin brothers in their cribs by the fire for a moment.

"This is our last chance. We had just started when the War between the States came and I had to take command of a cavalry troop. That's all over, thank heaven, but we have to make it now. It's either now, or I come home to punch cattle for someone else! There are eleven hundred steers down there in the valley, all we and two others can drive. We'll sell them up north and not have to worry."

Lance saw his mother touch her fingers to her eyes as she moved to the bedroom door. Later, when he thought about it, he wondered. In her bedroom, his mother was laying out the riding skirts, with their great flare and the hooks on the side so they could be caught up and not catch on brambles and briers as Lou Ann rode side-saddle.

It was too bad, Lance thought, that she couldn't ride astride like a boy. But ladies didn't ride that way. They were packing her chests and the medicine box. Lance lay in the bunk by the fireplace and

[*8*]

watched his father thumbing through the herd book. Then he felt his eyelids drooping . . . drooping . . .

The *clang-clang, clang-clang* of Juan's bell brought Lance out of bed and hurried him into

his clothes and boots in the early morning dark. In the yellow lantern light in the kitchen, he found his father talking with the men who would go with them. There stood tall and lean Travis Cantrell, the foreman; Juan Santiago, the Mexican cook; the horse herder, Zeke Terry; the big Negro puncher, Mitch Tally; the Indian, Harden Wright, and the three men from over west: Fitz Land, John Abbott, and Ed Davis.

They were good men and big men, and Lance liked them all. He watched his father draw a line across the page of the book where they listed the total of the steers, and he read: "Monday, March 2, 1868," at the top of the page.

"Eleven hundred steers, Lance, and all good ones!" Lance's father sipped his coffee. "Travis has one hundred and fifty. Fifty belong to Harden Wright. All wear our 'Box C' brand for the drive up the Chisholm Trail. Here, you keep the tally book, Lance. If we have any losses, you put them down. Be sure of your arithmetic!"

Just at first gray daylight, Lance kissed his mother good-by, then climbed into the saddle on his paint horse. This was the start up the Chisholm Trail! Quickly, he rode after Travis Cantrell and Harden Wright, down over the edge of the plateau into the valley to the east. They dragged enough of the stickery brush and the mesquite away to make a gate in the brush fence. First came the trail cow, the only cow they would have with them, then the steers, single-filing behind her.

"Lance! Hey, Lance!" Travis Cantrell called to him. "Here comes Mitch Tally! He's your pardner. You two are riding 'drag'!"

Out of the tangled mass of steers, Mitch Tally's pinto worked his way like a toe dancer, jumping sideways, until he reached the brush gate where Lance waited.

"Mitch!" Lance called over the rattling of steer horns and the sound of steers lowing. "What's 'drag'? Travis says I'm your pardner."

"I'll tell you, Lance, sure enough!" Mitch moved his pinto closer. "Way out in front there'll be Juan Santiago and Miss Lou Ann. Off to one side or the other, there'll be Zeke Terry with the remuda, all the extra horses in the herd. Your papa and Travis Cantrell will ride 'point' and guide the herd. Harden Wright and John Abbott will ride 'swing' so's to help turn the herd along the trail. Fitz Land and Ed Davis, they've got to ride 'flank,' so's we can keep the herd following the point and swing. We've got to ride the 'drag,' and that means we'll bring up the rear with all those pokey old steers. Means we got to eat that dust all the way up that old Chisholm Trail to Abilene, Kansas. We got to work up some way. By and by, we get to ride point on a herd, unless we get too old!" Mitch slapped a leather-covered leg and rocked with laughter. "We'll be old enough, time we reach Abilene!"

Lance watched through the early dawn as the punchers brought the last of the steers through the gate in the brush fence. He could see the steam from the steers' damp, heated bodies and hear the punchers shouting their high-pitched "Hiiiie! Hiiiie! Hiiiie!" over the clacking of horns, the snorting, and the popping of hoofs. For a moment, Lance felt a little fear. There were so many steers, more than he had ever worked. Maybe that was it, he thought—no difference, only more!

"Lance!" Travis Cantrell rode quickly through the brush gate. "This herd is cold and spooky. Watch out! It will take a day or so before they become trail smart. Help Mitch!"

"There's my old spooky steer, Lance!" Mitch swung the end of his lariat at a big, rangy beast with a set of horns almost seven feet in length. "Been started up the Chisholm Trail three times! Got away every time!"

Slowly, slowly, turning to left and to right, Lance and Mitch kept the tail-end of the herd moving down the valley to the east, grazing as it went. Lance's father rode back to join them where the valley widened. Far ahead, Lance could see Juan's chuck wagon and Lou Ann's smaller wagon following the old road by the river. The big herd was strung out for over a mile, a long, wide stain on the green grass of the river valley.

"Take us about seventy days, Lance, maybe less with no trouble." Lance's father called to him. "We'll cover about seven hundred miles of the thousand that make the Chisholm Trail, if you count from the Rio Grande. Could push faster, but the steers have good winter tallow on. If we hurried, we would walk it off them. This way, we'll have good prime beef when we reach Abilene up in Kansas. Ten miles a day! It's been a good winter in the Indian Nation country, and the grass is fine."

[*13*]

By high noon, the wind had driven the scudding clouds away, and the sun came down hot through the moist air. Lance stopped just long enough to scoop up a hatbrim of water from a cold spring. Then he rode on, munching the biscuit and veal steak sandwich from his saddle bag. Later, Mitch told him to find Zeke and change horses. He waved to Lou Ann as the two wagons pulled away along the river road to find a place for the night. Tomorrow, they would be in San Antonio or close by. They'd buy a bell for the trail cow. He was to buy a new rain sheet, a poncho, for himself. When they reached the Indian Nation country, Papa said he and Lou Ann could visit with Mr. Jesse Chisholm himself! Lance felt a shiver of excitement. This wasn't work, he thought. This was fun! Even so, it was man's work on the trail.

The trail, Chisholm's Trail! Lance remembered what his father had told him about the trail, and about Mr. Chisholm. He'd been a government freighter, Mr. Chisholm had, carrying supplies and food and clothing and ammunition to the military forts up in Indian Territory. And he had been a trader with the Indian tribes.

And sometimes, he was the one who made treaties and agreements for the government with the tribes. Mr. Chisholm was the only one the Indians would trust. And everywhere he went, Jesse Chisholm had marked his trail, finding the easy places for his horses and wagons, and finding the crossings over the creeks and rivers. That had been important because it was wild country and no one had any maps with which to find their way.

Way back before the Civil War, Jesse Chisholm had traded all through the Indian Country with the various tribes, and his wagons had carried supplies for other traders. Just after the big war had started, a tribe of Indians, the Wichitas, who wanted to stay with the Union, or Northern, side in the Civil War, and who were having trouble with other tribes who did not, asked Jesse Chisholm to guide them to safe country in Kansas. He agreed, and he led them back over the wagon trails he had made delivering supplies and trading. Later, when Mr. McCoy came to him and asked him to mark a trail for the cattle drives to come up from Texas, it was easy. He remembered the trails he had made to the various traders and when he had gone down to the big Red River to lead the

Wichita Tribe to safety. When he had talked with Mr. McCoy, he had started southward over his old trails and marked a trail for the Calhoun herd that Mr. McCoy had bought, so the cattle drivers could find their way north from Texas to the end of the trails and the railroads in Kansas.

An hour before dusk, Lance could see the herd commence to mill round and round in a slowly moving coil where his father and Travis Cantrell had decided to bed the steers for the night. It was almost dark when Lance and Mitch Tally pushed the lazy ones of the drag into the bedding ground. The valley was wide here. There was good grass, and there was water from the river. Already two of the punchers were walking their horses slowly around the edges of the herd as it quieted for the night.

Lance saw his father signal from the far side of the herd, and he put the little pinto into a lope and circled toward the riverbank. As the pinto turned past a plum thicket, Lance thought he saw something move. Once beyond it, he was sure! It was Mitch Tally's spooky steer racing for the river!

Without thinking, Lance had his lariat in his

[*16*]

hands and was guiding the pinto after the steer with his knees. The pinto squealed and jumped after the steer like a rabbit as it dodged toward the river. A tree limb jerked Lance's hat back on its throat latch, and briers tore at his batwing chaps. Just short of the high bank of the river, they caught up with the racing steer. Lance flipped the loop of his lariat out and down over the steer's horns, head, and neck. The next instant the pinto had started to swing back to safe ground to brace himself, but it was too late!

The rope snubbed to the saddle horn snapped tight! Lance heard the pinto whicker wildly just before they cartwheeled high into the air and out and down toward the blackness of the dark river. As he turned through the air, Lance saw the spooky steer sail majestically out over the high riverbank like a big, big bird with enormous, wide horns for wings, legs aspraddle, bellowing. The water was cold and wet and choking by the time Lance realized what had happened. He felt the powerful, surging pressure of the river current, then he and the pinto were fighting madly toward the riverbank with his lariat still tight to the wild, spooky steer!

CHAPTER TWO

San Antonio Town

LANCE fought with all his strength to untie his lariat on the horn of the pinto's saddle. Just as the lariat came loose, he felt the little horse roll under the water. As he dog-paddled in the water, Lance could see the shadows of his father and Mitch Tally and their horses on the riverbank, and he heard Harden Wright, the Indian, call:

"Grab his tail, Lance! Grab his tail!"

Lance felt the pinto's tail fanned out in the water and caught a handful of hair. Then the pinto's hoofs touched bottom, and he commenced to heave himself through the shallow water toward the dark riverbank. Above, Lance heard the

[*18*]

singing of lariats reaching out toward the spooky steer in the tumbling river's water.

A minute's scramble at the riverbank and the pinto dragged Lance headlong to the dry ground near his father's black shadow in the twilight. The pinto was safe; he was safe, and the men had their lariats on the wild steer! Lance pushed to his knees and scrubbed the water and dry leaves from his face and jacket. Suddenly, he felt his stomach try to turn over. He reached up and caught the stirrup leathers on the pinto's saddle and pulled himself to his feet. He was trembling and the pinto was trembling, but they were both safe!

Later, as he sat by Juan Santiago's cookfire in his bedroll, Lance tried to tell Lou Ann what had happened. But—the fire was warm, the night a starlighted darkness. The soup and cornbread had filled his stomach, and it all seemed like something out of a bad dream. Without even saying "good night," Lance dozed off in a tired sleep.

The next day, an hour past the sun's noon shadow, Lance could make out the distant outline of San Antonio. Dust from the moving herd hazed the view, but it was there. Lance felt a stir of excitement as he turned the calico-colored horse he was riding to round up a lazy steer. San Antone, as his father called it, was the biggest town for miles and miles in that part of Texas.

Two hours later, Lance and Mitch Tally were pushing the last of the drag in a wide curve fol-

lowing the lead around the town toward the dark clump of trees beside a creek and the night's bedding ground. As he worked, Lance looked when he could at the vast, sprawling town of little square houses with flat roofs. They looked as if they were

made of mud, but he remembered it was called adobe. Standing by some of the houses and at the ends of the wide streets were women with babies slung over their hips, and little boys and girls watching, and here and there men on horseback sitting quietly. This is a herd on the move, Lance thought, and he was proud to be a part of a drive up the Chisholm Trail!

As he and Mitch pushed the last of the herd across the sprawling creek, Lance could see Zeke Terry's rope fence up at the head of the valley to hold the horses. The steers were already slowing down into a quiet, cud-chewing herd moving clocklike in the middle of the valley. Near a spring, Lance and Mitch found Juan's chuck wagon and Lou Ann's spring-bed wagon. A fire had been made for cooking and for the night, wood gathered, and half the punchers were now cleaning up and dressing for the trip into town. Lance felt like giving a wild yell but saw his father watching him, a smile on his lips. Lou Ann came running as he slid down from his saddle.

"Harden Wright, Zeke, and Mitch will stay with the herd, Lance, until you and some of the others come back from town," Colonel Calhoun said. "Lou Ann has to buy some lady-stuff. You're to buy a rain sheet, and you'd better buy some more breeches." Lance busied himself slinging his saddle and blanket and the bridle over the limb of a gnarled old tree. He'd ride the pinto into town. "You take first watch tonight, son. Juan will drive in for supplies. May rain, so watch out!"

In spite of the darkness, the gathering clouds, and the fitful wind, Lance and Lou Ann were happy. And the happiness mounted as they rode through the darkness with Lance's father and the punchers beside the creaking and heavy shadow of Juan's chuck wagon.

They were aware of the feathery shadows of willow and the gaunt pictures of towering oaks as they rode along. Ahead, Lance could see a dimness of lights against the darkness. Then he could make out the dark silhouettes of adobe houses, a church with its cross outlined against the night. His horse stumbled, and Lance realized the road was deep-rutted and uneven. He saw more houses looming up in the night and a cross street. Far ahead, he could make out the lights he had seen from a distance, some in the windows of houses and some shining through the larger windows of stores. And beyond, he could see the shadowy loom of bigger buildings. There were horses tethered at hitching racks in front of the buildings. Lance could hear the sound of voices and of laughter. "This is San Antonio!" Lance thought. "This is the big town."

"Oh, look, there's the Alamo!" Lou Ann had seen the big fort when she came to visit the Calhouns, but Lance never had. "And there's the cathedral, and the stores!" Lance was all eyes as they turned in to the hitch rack before a big store. Lights and windows and doors and people! Lance had

[*24*]

never seen so many. And there was noise—people laughing and people singing, and the sweet notes of a guitar.

"Look, Lance, look at the lady with the big comb in her hair! She's so pretty!" Lou Ann exclaimed.

While a clerk waited on Lou Ann, Juan was busy at another counter, then Lance found a clerk to help him. He tried on the great square of oiled canvas with the hole in the middle to put his head through, then he bought four pairs of denim breeches, and, after he spoke to the clerk, they found a delicately carved tortoise shell comb for Lou Ann. But that was a surprise for long later in Abilene.

His father met Lance at the wide doorway as they carried the supplies out to Juan's chuck wagon. As Lance stood waiting for Lou Ann, his father thrust a parcel into his hand.

"Man-sized spurs, son! Put them on!"

All the way through the darkness to the bedding ground, Lance could hear the faint music of the spur rowels singing in the night. Soon they reached the herd, Juan's heavily laden wagon groaning in its turn by the flickering firelight, and Lou Ann hurrying to her wagon with her packages and bundles. Lance felt two inches taller as he stuffed his purchases into his bedroll and hurried off to relieve Harden Wright. New spurs —man-sized spurs!

In spite of the gusts of wind and the rain clouds that bulged with lightning to the south, the herd remained quiet. As he walked the pinto slowly around the sleeping steers, Lance tried to sing the way he'd heard Travis Cantrell and his father and John Abbott sing, soft and soothing to keep them quiet, but it didn't sound the same. He sang anyway, for a while, some of the Mexican songs Juan had taught him. Then he sang some of the "Texas Cowboy."

"Oh, I am a Texas cowboy, far away from home.
If I ever get back to Texas I nevermore will roam."

Then he said to himself, "That isn't the kind of a song to sing on the Chisholm Trail. There's the 'Old Chisholm Trail Song.' It's a sad song, but all the trail songs are sad." For a moment he tried to remember the song as Juan had sung it time and time again around the bunkhouse and in the kitchen at the house.

"Come along, boys, and listen to my tale,
I'll tell you of my troubles on the old Chisholm trail.
  Coma ti yi youpy, youpy yea, youpy yea,
  Coma ti yi youpy, youpy yea.

"Oh, a ten-dollar hoss and a forty-dollar saddle,
And I'm goin' to punchin' Texas cattle.
I'm up in the mornin' afore daylight
And afore I sleep the moon shines bright.
Oh, it's bacon and beans most every day—
I'd as soon be a-eatin' prairie hay."

It grew late and he felt drowsy, but he stayed awake, watching the lightning, feeling the touch of rain showers on the new rain sheet Juan called a "poncho," watching for a restless move in the herd.

Lance was near the upper end of the valley just below Zeke's horse herd when he heard the sound of horses and heard Lou Ann's call, soft but urgent:

"Lance . . . Lance!"

He turned back and found her at the edge of the dark tree shadows, sitting bareback on the little Barb mare.

"Trouble, Lance! Be quiet!" she whispered to him. "After Harden and Zeke and Mitch left, three men came. I could hear them shouting at Juan

and demanding money and saying they were going to run off our cattle!"

He couldn't find Ed Davis on the far side of
the herd without giving himself away. Lance
motioned to Lou Ann and drifted away in the
shadows of the trees around the sleeping herd toward the chuck wagon. His carbine was in the
chuck wagon. Juan needed help!

"Lou!" he whispered. "Get down. Let's walk
from here." When she joined him, he leaned close
to her. "Get your little shotgun. I'll find something and come up on the far side. I'll find something!"

"I can't shoot a man, Lance. I can't!"

As he crawled into the dim shadow near the
chuck wagon, Lance wondered what to do. Near
the fire, he could make out a towering big man,
and two smaller ones, then the figure of Juan,
writhing and fighting, bent over the flames of the
cook fire. He could hear the big man laugh and
hear Juan's cry. They were burning him like
Indians!

Looped over the brake handle of the chuck
wagon, Lance spied the coils of Juan's bull whip
in the flickering light of the fire. His hand tugged

at it, and it slithered to the ground. Beyond the fire, in the shadows, Lance could see Lou Ann standing by her wagon, the little shotgun in her hands.

Juan was fighting the two smaller men, tugging at their arms around his shoulders, and suddenly he broke free. Lance saw Lou Ann's shotgun come up, saw the violent blaze of fire from its muzzles . . . one . . . two, saw the coals and fire and ashes of Juan's fire explode high into the night and shower down over the two as Juan scrambled away. Lance lifted the whip as Juan had taught him, flung it back and forward, to wrap it around the shoulders and stomach of the big, laughing man.

He heard the man cry out, then felt himself jerked forward like a stone from a slingshot straight for the bed of glimmering coals of fire. As his arms came up to shield his face, he heard the harsh voice of Harden Wright shouting a command!

CHAPTER THREE

Wild Horses

THE night was a jumble of wild sounds as Lance fought against the pull of the whip and the man fighting to escape into the darkness. As he was dragged along the ground, Lance could see the two smaller men rolling on the ground, slapping at the embers on their clothes and shouting. He fought back against the leather thong looped around his wrist.

"Hold it!" His father's hand lifted him to his feet, and as he dared look he saw that the shadowy space around the fire was ringed with faces, some on horseback, some on foot, all friends. Juan held Lou Ann in the crook of his arm, and she still held the little double-barreled shotgun. Near the fire the two men still slapped at burning places in their clothes. The big man lay quiet, hands lifted, looking at Harden Wright and the long pistol he held in his hand.

"Get up!" the Indian ordered.

Lance saw three deputy sheriffs riding up as he hurried to Lou Ann and Juan.

"Oh, Lance, I couldn't shoot people. I—I just shot the fire and closed my eyes." Lance felt like laughing and couldn't. "It was so awful for Juan."

"Leetle one is all right . . ." Juan held Lou Ann close. "This one is like iron skillet—just needs hand to help."

Suddenly the stormy night was filled with laughter as the punchers slapped Lance on the back and patted Lou Ann's shoulder, then joined the ring around the three thieves. Harden had thrown more wood on the fire, and it blazed up, making the night yellowish.

The deputies put their hands on the three men and dragged them away, heading toward San Antonio. Lance looked at Lou Ann.

"You all right, Lou?"

"My shotgun needs cleaning, and I wish your mother was here!"

Lance wished it, too, but he was wearing man-sized spurs now, and he'd have to toe a line by himself. He heard his father help Lou Ann into her wagon as he found his bedroll, and, later, as he worked his way into the blankets, he felt the cool touch of the first drops of rain.

In the days that followed, the herd became trail wise. The old cow, wearing her new bell proudly, clanged her way along, following Lance's father and Travis Cantrell, the foreman. Even the spooky steer which had tumbled Lance into the river became more gentle and seemed to seek out Lance to stand by. Once or twice, Lance thought the steer was following him as he rode. By this time, the herd was deep in the cross-timber country with its thickets and rolling hills and deep gulches. It was different from the brush country, with more open spaces, but with more heavy timber and ranches closer together, and little cross-trails where there were people to watch the first herd of the year head north up the Chisholm Trail.

Late one afternoon, when Lance and Mitch Tally pushed their lazy drag over the crest of a high ridge, they found his father, Travis Cantrell, and Harden Wright talking with an old hunter. He sat astride a great claybank horse, the saddle bags on his Mexican saddle bulging, as were the packs tied behind him. Across the horn of his saddle, he balanced an old-time long rifle. The men were listening with care as the old man talked and gestured with his hands, making sweeping circles in the air and pointing behind him to the west.

Lance felt he was all eyes for he couldn't help watching the old hunter. This must be one of the mountain men he had heard so much about. They were the hunters who went, sometimes by themselves, sometimes in groups of five or ten, all the way up into the Rocky Mountains way off to the northwest. And they traded with the Indians and trapped for furs, and just wandered all over. They were mighty brave to go so far by themselves. Lance shivered at the thought, then he looked closely at the long rifle and saw the great knife in its sheath at his belt. Mitch moved up to Lance's side.

"I hear tell that one of those mountain hunters can just walk right up to a grizzly bear and hug him flat just like a pancake." Mitch ruffled his

horse's mane. "Reckon he's sure got some news for the colonel."

As anxious as he was to hear what the hunter had to say, he did not want to go near until his

father signaled to him. He and Mitch turned their horses into the remuda and hung their saddles in the forks of two trees off the ground. Lance spoke to Mitch as they scrubbed at the trail dust on their faces and hands.

"Wish I was bigger or older so I could know just where we are. All I know is we are so many days up the trail. But, where is that?"

"I'm older and I'm bigger," Mitch laughed. "But, me, I don't know more than you at all."

That evening they held a council of war, all of them except Fitz Land and Ed Davis, who were riding night herd. Lance's father swept a place clean on the ground near Juan's fire and scratched a map with a stick.

"That old hunter said the Plains Indians have pushed the wild herds down into the cross-timbers where we are. They'll try to steal our horses. And they may spook our cattle, particularly if they come at night!" Lance shivered at the thought. "Double night herd, and everyone watch. Everyone!"

Twice, as he rode the calico or a paint Zeke had given him as a third horse, Lance thought he saw something in the brush near the drag. A

third time, the calico horse had called to something on the slope of the valley west of them as
they rode along.

"Nothing but a coyote on the prowl," Mitch
yelled back at Lance. "Woods full of creepy
things!"

Came a day when the wind swung to the north
and a late blue norther drove down on them, a
wet, cold wind whistling out of the north, the
clouds all purplish-blue and hugging the earth,
cutting their faces and hands. Everyone had to
dig deep for heavy coats and gloves. By night,
the wind was spitting cold raindrops and sleet,
and the temperature dropped so quickly that
Lance added his poncho just to give some warmth
to the horse he rode. As it turned darker, the
wind blew harder and became wilder. Only Lou
Ann and Juan bedded down that night. The rest
hunched down around Juan's fire and thought
about the men riding night herd.

"Anything happen, it will happen tonight!"
Travis Cantrell broke the silence. "This night's
made for trouble."

Through the whining wind, the men crouched
around the fire could hear the cry of a lobo wolf

back on the hill to the west, an eerie call that made the horses snort. Lance felt the skin on the back of his neck tighten, and a chill crept over his shoulders. Somewhere up the hill Zeke was talking to his horses, Lance knew, and two men rode round and round the herd. When midnight came, he would have to go out there, and he shivered at the thought.

"Get some sleep, son," Lance heard his father say and felt him touch his shoulder. "It's a bad night, and we may all be up before morning!"

Lance felt he had hardly rolled into his blankets when he heard Harden Wright's demanding call. He fought his way out of the bedroll, dragged at his boots, and was worrying at his spur straps when he heard Lou Ann's whisper by his side.

"What is it, Lance, what is it?"

He didn't know, no one knew. Quickly, he ran for his saddle and blanket and bridle, then to the picketed pinto under the trees. The pinto took a deep breath, and Lance put his knee against his stomach and hauled tight on the saddle girt. Let a saddle turn and there would be trouble. He saw the dim shadow of someone ahead of him as he rode around the herd, which was just now commencing to get to its feet and to show signs of restlessness. Don't let them stampede; don't let them stampede, thought Lance, as he rode.

As he rounded the herd of steers moving restlessly on his left, Lance could see and hear riders moving ahead of him. Soon he joined Mitch and Travis Cantrell as they headed up the valley. The little pinto was nervous when they halted just below the edge of the valley rim.

"Harden and John Abbott saw a stallion on the rim of the valley awhile ago calling to Zeke's remuda bunch!" Ed Davis said, turning in his saddle. "He was a fire-eating broncho, if ever I heard one!"

Just then Lance heard a high, piercing whistle, an answering whicker, then the resounding thud of hoofs pouring down over the rim of the valley. It was impossible to see in the darkness; they just had to sense their way. But they had to head the wild horses away from Zeke's horse herd or they would be afoot within two days.

Travis called to Lance in the darkness. "Follow me! This way!"

Quickly, they threaded their way through some briery brush into an opening where the wind and rain and sleet caught them full in the face. Just then Lance heard the whistle of a stallion and saw the wild herd flowing down toward them. He heard Travis' gun bellow, saw its flash, and saw the shadow of the herd swing to their right. Then he was shouting, yelling, and the others joined him. The wild ones came close to Zeke's herd in its rope corral, then plunged off in the night, leaving a rumble of hoofs and wild whickers.

Out of the darkness on his right, Lance sensed more than saw the towering shape of the wild stallion which had led the herd. He felt the pinto spin to the right, then gather himself and lunge. As he moved, Lance whipped the loop of his lariat high into the air and leaned low in the saddle away from the screaming horse. The pinto ran free for an instant, then Lance felt the rope tighten on the horn of the saddle. He felt the pinto set himself to brace against the rope. It was so dark, and there was no one near when Lance felt the surge of the wild stallion and heard his scream. Then the rope slipped on the horn of his saddle. Lance felt the pinto bounce backward as his head smashed into the limb of a tree in the darkness.

CHAPTER FOUR

The Long Spears

LANCE lay stunned for a moment, then he remembered the pinto. He raised his head but could see nothing in the darkness, and he could hear nothing but the wind moaning through the trees. He felt the grass, and he lay back and tried to see against the light of the skyline. Suddenly, he heard a soft whicker behind him, and he crawled toward it on his hands and knees. It was the pinto.

He could feel his soft muzzle and his warm breath. In the darkness he could just make out the body of the pinto, bottom side up, feet in the air, wedged between two trees. He called into the night, but no one heard him. For a moment, he

[*41*]

was afraid. Then he heard the pinto whicker to him again.

"Good boy. We'll be out of here in a minute!"

Lance crawled around the trees beside him and found the pinto's tail. He wound a big hank of hair in his gloved hands, set his heels, and pulled. He pulled once, twice, felt the pinto slip, roll to one side, then he pulled again. He heard the horse mumbling to himself, and he pulled again. Just as the pinto rolled to his feet, he heard his father and Harden Wright calling to him.

"This way!" he answered. "We're over here!"

They made their way through the trees, through the wild wind and the rain that had commenced to drive down again. Lance felt the little pinto all over to see if he was all right. He told them what had happened.

"Your rope's gone, boy!" Travis spoke suddenly. "If that horse has your rope on him, he may trap himself!"

Lance hadn't thought of that, and in a moment he was off down the hill slope, dragging the pinto behind him. Even a wild horse deserves some help if he is in trouble. They combed the trees and the grassy openings, and where the slope broke into

"Lance! Slip up and loosen your lariat!"

the valley, they found the stallion tangled in Lance's rope and the rope snarled around the base of a willow.

The stallion was beautiful even in the vague light the night gave them, and Lance wished more than anything that the horse could be his. Slowly and cautiously, his father and Travis dropped their lariats over the straining horse and backed away.

"Lance! Slip up and loosen your lariat!"

For an instant, he hesitated. He wanted the big horse, but his father had spoken. Quietly, Lance crept up to the stallion, loosened the noose of his rope until he could throw it over and behind the horse's hind quarters. Then he scurried for the deeper darkness of the trees. Quickly, his father and Travis flipped their lariats loose and away. For a long moment, the stallion just stood, breathing deep, making noises in his throat. Suddenly, he whistled, spun high on his hind legs, and galloped away.

"I know, son," Lance's father said quietly, "but he's a wild one. You wouldn't want him."

By morning the creek near where they had bedded was a raging torrent of muddy water, and it was not until the second day that they were able to send the herd over the ford and on along the trail. By noontime, the sun had come out, and the earth steamed with its heat. Gradually the going became easier, and for a day lost, they had made a day, a long day in which they pushed on to a big spring and good grass for the night's bedding.

Everything was sopping wet, so that night they slept on top of their ground sheets and hung their blankets on bushes to dry. It was work from "can see" at earliest daylight to "can't see" after twilight for the next week, until Lance felt he could not ride any more. He couldn't walk, he couldn't sit, and he couldn't sleep, he was so tired.

"You should take a day off and go fishing!" Lou Ann had remarked with a smile, and Lance laughed as he dozed off one night. Fish? He had work to do.

They had made half the day's drive, the herd lined out as far as the eye could follow it along the slope of a valley that led always north, when they saw strangers on horses riding toward the herd. Lance's father and John Abbott rode off to meet them. They pulled up and sat talking for a while. Lance saw one of the men make an angry gesture, then turn and ride away. As darkness drew on, John Abbott rode back to the drag as Mitch and Lance pushed them into a meadow near a bend in the creek.

"Man wanted to go in ahead of us. Said he had a right to be ahead. Colonel Calhoun said no! Man forgot his manners, and that ended that!"

Lance thought of his mother and her remarks about manners all the time, and he wondered if she ever had to talk to his father about manners. If the stranger had gone ahead, the grass would be hard to find, the waters muddied. Besides, the Calhoun "Box C" was first up the Chisholm Trail this year, and it should be first!

As Lance swung away from the bedded herd, the spooky steer followed him and the calico pony he rode. At first, the steer was hesitant—walking a few steps, pausing, then a few more, until Lance was surprised to look up from his plate of beans and cornbread where he sat talking with Lou Ann to find the steer standing within a dozen feet, just watching.

"Go away!" Lance said and gestured with his fork. "Go away!"

But when Lance changed saddle to the paint horse Zeke had given him, the spooky steer watched him from the edge of the bedded herd and followed him as he rode off to relieve Fitz Land. It was dark by the time he reached the far side of the herd, and yet Lance knew his friend the spooky steer was not far behind him. It was not right; one walking steer could set the whole herd milling around, and that meant trouble.

As he made his round, Lance found the steer had left him, but when he reached the far side near the slope of the valley, he found the steer again. He was facing the valley wall and snorting. Lance stopped his horse. What was he to do? In the starlight, he could make out the steer, the trees, the valley wall. But what was the steer snorting about? Slowly, the steer edged closer to him, always watching the trees up the valley, and snuffing the light wind.

As he made the next round, John Abbott met him and told him about the spooky steer standing all by himself in the dark. And Lance told him about the steer following him around day after day and that night.

"You have a friend!" John Abbott laughed.

[*47*]

"But don't let him spook this herd, Lance!"

By this time, the near-full moon had come up, flooding all the valley and the meadow in which the herd bedded with its rich, full light. And as the man and the boy made their slow turns around the herd the spooky steer was always waiting at the head of the valley, watching the trees. The next time around, Lance slid from his saddle and found Harden Wright in the row of sleeping punchers.

"Mr. Wright! Harden!" he whispered to the sleeping Indian. The next instant he was looking down the barrel of a long Colt revolver! "Please! That steer's followed me and won't leave the trees at the upper end of the valley!" Suddenly he felt a need for urgency. "Harden, please get up! That steer knows something!"

Quickly, without a moment's loss of time, Harden Wright was up and pulling on his clothes and boots. As they rode around the herd, Lance saw Harden pull his pistol, then work the action of his carbine.

"Lance, go back quietly and rouse your father and everyone. Tell your father it 'smells' like Indians."

[*48*]

The paint horse moved swiftly and quietly through the night like a shadow. At the chuck wagon it was the work of a moment to speak to his father, and quickly everyone was awake. Lance heard his father whispering to Travis, then the word was passed on down to all the others. Like shadows, each one picked up the gear he wanted

and drifted away to find his saddle and his horse picketed near by. He heard Juan scratch on Lou Ann's canvas wagon cover, and he wanted to go speak to her, but there was work to do. He turned the paint horse back up the valley and followed his father.

It seemed only a moment until they were grouped near the spooky steer. Almost like a whisper on the wind, Lance heard Harden Wright's instructions.

"Spread out, right and left. Hold your fire! There are Indians up the slope!"

Almost as he spoke, Lance heard a wild yell that rent the moonlit night and seemed to freeze him to the marrow of his bones. The next instant, he heard the rumble of hoofs pouring down into the valley, the thunder of rifles and handguns, and he saw the spooky steer charge a horseman riding straight for him! And the horseman held a spear in his hand!

Lance turned and dug his spurs into the paint horse to ride up beside his father. Just then the spooky steer's horns met the Indian's horse. The night was filled with flailing hoofs, the sound of carbines, an Indian's wild yell, the steer's mad bellow, and the scream of the paint horse as they all rolled down the slope.

CHAPTER FIVE

The Little Warrior

For a long, long moment, there was the rumble of horses' hoofs, then the noises faded and Lance discovered he could see things again. There was his father, and Travis Cantrell, and way to the side, there was Harden Wright, but no one else!

He heard his father call, then silence. For a moment, no one answered, then the queerest thing—one by one, he heard a hooty owl, the chirruping of a ground squirrel, and the sound of a mourning dove—one right after the other.

"They're all right, son! Don't worry." Lance's father whispered to him. "Just keep quiet—"

Lance heard the soft steps of horses in the shadows. Then, one by one, the punchers drifted into the moonlight.

"Should have known they might come when the moon was out," said Harden Wright. He rode close to Lance's father. "They're the ones put the wild horses onto us. When that didn't work, they came down on us in a moonlight raid!"

All of a sudden, Lance shivered. Then he remembered the spooky steer.

"Papa! Papa!" Lance spoke suddenly to his father. "If it hadn't been for the spooky steer, we never would have been ready for the Indians—"

"That's right," Harden Wright answered in the shadows. "Lance woke me, and that was the first thing he said."

"You mean the spooky steer smelled the Indians first?" Lance's father turned in his saddle. "You mean . . ." His voice trailed off into the night.

"The old spooky steer followed me like a dog all evening after I relieved Fitz Land. Finally he just stayed right here and snuffed and wouldn't move. That was when I went back to the chuck wagon and woke up Harden and you and everybody—"

Suddenly Travis Cantrell and Mitch Tally were bent over their saddles laughing, and Lance wondered if he should have spoken about the spooky steer.

"Should have trained that steer to hunt birds or something," said Travis. "Or put a saddle on him and used him on this drive." Then they laughed some more.

Day after long day, the herd moved northward. Below Austin, Lance's father and Travis Cantrell had swung the herd to the west and forded the Colorado River at a ford when the high waters had gone down. And they had waited for two days for the Leon River to drop to where they could cross it. It took a long, long time to make a trail drive, thought Lance, and this was only a part of the way. But he remembered what Travis had told him. They were still the first herd up the trail that year!

It was on the fifth day beyond the Leon River that Harden Wright said he was going to hunt for some fresh meat. Harden always rode like a cavalry soldier, tall and straight in the saddle, big hat square on his head. He had his carbine at the ready when he rode away from the herd.

It must have been three hours later by the sun when Lance saw the tall Indian across the valley to the east, a deer carcass bouncing against his legs on the saddle.

Lance could sense the excitement as he rode toward Ed Davis, riding the flank above him. Then he saw John Abbott wave to Travis, and soon his father and Travis came swinging back toward them.

"That man that wanted to move in ahead of us ten days ago is trying to cut us off from the east." Harden came galloping up to them. "I saw him an hour ago. He's pushing his herd to get ahead of us. There's a creek that flows at the base of that cliff you can see north of us. He's trying to round that ahead of us!"

Lance's father turned in his saddle and sat looking for a moment, then he spoke quietly.

"Have to push. We need all the good grass we can get, and he won't leave us much ahead from here north. Harden, give that meat to Juan and tell all the boys to move along as fast as they can. We're driving straight ahead, and that fellow will have to make a curve. We'll still be ahead of him!"

Some of the punchers had told Lance how important it was to keep ahead on the trail. Each herd that went up the trail left a little less grass for the next fellow. Sometimes there wouldn't be much water in the water holes, and the first herd wouldn't leave enough for the next. Then he remembered his father telling him how important it was to be the first to reach the cattle market, if you had not already sold. And then there was just the fun of being first, of winning. Sometimes, men who were mean tried to mix their herds up with others so they might possibly be able to steal a few extra steers, even if they were branded for the trail.

Far and away, Lance could make out the gleam of sunlight on the covers of Juan's and Lou Ann's wagons as they moved far ahead of the point of the herd. A lagging steer made a dash for a plum thicket, and Lance had to drive headlong after him, his arms raised to protect his eyes, his horse squealing at the pricks of the thorns. By the time he had turned the steer back into the herd, the drag was below the crest of a long hill, and Lance could no longer see the point. By this time in the day, the dust was commencing to rise, and the steers talked deep in their throats as they were pushed along the trail. Lance wondered if they

[55]

were going to make it ahead of the other herd and looked at the hot sun and wished the day were over.

They pushed on that afternoon, harder than ever. They crossed the shallows over the creek below the edge of the plateau while the sun was two hours high. Beyond the creek, the land mounted higher, and soon they were on a kind of hump of land with clumps of trees and thick grass. Lance found the signs of an old trail and a spot where a campfire had been made.

As they crested the hump of land and moved on to the level beyond, Lance looked back and saw, far behind, the lifting dust of the herd that had tried to cut them off. Lance felt a yell inside and lifted his puncher's hat and waved it at Ed Davis and saw him wave his hat at Travis Cantrell. His father knew they had won. Twilight was close on them, but it was still clear except for the towering clouds rolling up from the Gulf to the south. Lance didn't think of that very much until he saw a cloud bulge heavy with lightning, then he hurried to round up his part of the drag. As always, now, the spooky steer followed him as he rode from one side to the other of the drag.

The point of the herd was bedding down beyond a wide, sprawling creek when Lance and Mitch brought the drag over a slight roll in the land. Lance sat his horse and watched for a moment. He could see the big herd moving slowly, clockwise, and beyond, the flicker of Juan's cook fire. Then he watched the drag of the herd he had been working with Mitch all day long moving slowly in until they were lost in the great circle of steers.

It was his turn to stay with the herd until Mitch came back. He started his slow walk around the herd. He tried to sing some of the songs John Abbott had taught him. It was still not quite dark. Then he discovered the spooky steer was following him again—two steps, then stop—three steps, then stop! Lance laughed to himself. Just like a dog, almost.

They had made their way nearly around the herd when Lance saw the steer peering into the thickets on the side of the creek above them. He heard the steer snuff, and watched him shake his widespread horns. Lance went on his slow ride around the dozing herd. By the time he had returned, Lance thought, the steer would be gone.

[57]

But he was still there watching the thicket, a blacker shadow in the shadows of the night. Lance paused, then moved his calico pony closer and leaned over to look into the thicket. Nothing there! Nothing he could see. So Lance commenced his circle again.

On the far side of the sleeping herd, Lance remembered the night the Indians came down on the herd, and the way the spooky steer had acted that night. As he made the turn past Juan's cook fire, Lance motioned to Harden Wright and moved on.

It was dark up the valley from the cook fire, dark and kind of scary now. Lance kept looking behind him, and he couldn't see Harden following him. He felt the calico pony quicken step and held him back with the reins. Suddenly Lance found himself beside the spooky steer.

Lance pulled the carbine from its boot and slid down from the saddle. He walked around the steer, and stood staring into the darkness of the thicket. Suddenly he felt the steer breathing on his shoulder and wished that Harden or someone was there. It was so dark and so lonesome.

Finally, he pulled the hammer back on the carbine and stepped slowly toward the thicket—one step—two steps—until he was about ten paces from the thicket. He saw nothing, but the spooky steer at his shoulder snorted at the thicket. There must be something there. Lance didn't know what to do. Then he heard a horse's soft step and knew that Harden Wright was behind him in the darkness.

Lance stepped forward and heard the steer move with him. Another step, another. Lance stood still.

Suddenly, out of the dark shadows, a lighter shadow moved. As his eyes bored into the darkness, Lance finally made out the slim shape of a small boy. He was naked from the waist up, but wore breech clout, leggings, and moccasins. Then Lance saw the great, tall spear the boy carried, and he raised the carbine.

"Lance! Don't shoot!" Harden exclaimed, and Lance dropped the muzzle of the carbine and waited. "It's just a little boy—"

Lance heard the big puncher come up behind him, then go past him and the steer.

"A little warrior—" Lance moved up beside Harden and looked into the darkness. It was just a little boy, with a great big spear. Lance leaned over and put the carbine on the ground and lifted his hands. He knew the Indian ways Harden and Juan had taught him. He saw the little warrior

put the spear point down, then lay it on the grass at his feet. "Friends . . . friends . . ." He heard Harden speak in two different languages. He heard the little warrior answer. Suddenly Harden was reaching out his arms.

The little Indian boy turned and led the way into the darkness of the thicket. Lance followed, and he saw the form of a woman, a young woman, lying on the ground, wrapped in a blanket. She was saying something he couldn't understand, and he saw the little Indian boy kneel by her side. Harden bent over the girl, then looked up at Lance and at the puzzled steer.

"I'll take her down to your father and Miss Lou Ann, Lance. This Indian girl is sick." Harden listened to her words. "They escaped from the Comanches who tried to raid us . . . a week . . . ten days ago . . . she has a fever . . . she says they are coming back!"

CHAPTER SIX

The Night the Wind Walked

SHE sure is sick, Harden!" Lance touched his hand to her forehead the way his mother did. "She's burning up with fever!"

She was beautiful, Lance thought. Older than Lou Ann and not so old as his mother. He scrambled from his knees to pull the poncho from his saddle.

"Wrap her in this. Her blanket and this rain sheet will keep her warm."

He watched the tall, slender form of Harden Wright straighten up. He held the young woman in his arms. How he managed to climb into the saddle with her weight, Lance could not understand. Then he stood watching Harden's horse move off toward the chuck wagon and Lou Ann. The little warrior, spear and all, trotted along beside him. Finally, there was just the spooky steer and Lance and his horse. He had work to do. He commenced his rounds again, and the steer followed behind him.

Lance had slept, eaten, and had worked the drag of the herd all day long before he was able to find out how the Indian lady fared. Lou Ann and Juan told him at supper.

"We gave her something Aunt Sarah put in the medicine chest, Lance," Lou Ann said. "It worked, and she is feeling better. They both slept all night and all day, they were so tired."

"And we make soup, such soup!" Juan added. "She eat it. So do leetle one with spear." Lou Ann giggled. "That spear, she is long and she is sharp. He is leetle *caballero*, leetle gentleman!"

The herd pushed on, with Lance's father and Travis leading the way. They crossed the flat lands, the easy fordings, finding the good bedding ground with grass and water for the herd. Lance lost count of the days and forgot time. They were near Fort Worth with the Brazos River crossing well behind them when the Indian lady first appeared. The fever was gone, and she smiled and spoke to Lance in English:

"Hello, friend Lance!"

Lance gulped his surprise and turned red when Lou Ann laughed at him. Then everyone laughed and it was a happy evening.

The little warrior sat close by and ate silently, watching with big brown eyes, a smile on his lips.

"Dove Song lived up near Boggy Depot in the Indian Country, Lance," Harden told him. "She and her little brother were captured by the Comanches on a raid. They escaped and you found them, just in time! Now, they are going to friends in Fort Worth, safely, this time."

Lance watched Harden's eyes. He had never seen the tall Indian so happy and kind of relaxed. Grown people were always different. Two days later, Travis and his father swung the herd in a wide arc to the west of Fort Worth. They would catch the Chisholm Trail again farther north beyond the big town. The next morning Juan and Lou Ann pulled their wagons off to the east. Dove Song and the little warrior rode beside Lou Ann and waved their hands as they disappeared from sight. Lou Ann would join them farther up the trail. Harden was riding with them. Lance shook his head and rode back to the herd.

As they topped a ridge, far to the east Lance could make out the buildings and houses of Fort Worth. He wished he could see it, but there wasn't time. They had to keep moving. Through the passing weeks, the herd had become a kind of trained company of steers, all except the spooky steer. He still followed Lance whenever he came near. But on this day, as they moved farther and farther northward into the rolling country north of Fort Worth, there was a kind of uneasiness in the herd.

Lance saw it, but decided he was wrong. Later Travis came riding back with John Abbott, standing in their stirrups to look over the herd.

"Better keep a close watch, boys!" Travis said as he joined Lance and Mitch. "Something in the weather, I guess. Wish Harden was back."

The weather was different, Lance realized. They had had the last norther days before, then long days of warmth and sunshine. Now it was hot, and the wind scurried around like puppies. Now it was quiet, now it blew this way and that. They pushed on, and that night Lance lay in his blankets and watched the clouds. They rolled up thick and heavy with darkness and lightning, muttering in the night. The next morning, the bellcow was switching her tail and eyeing things Lance could not see. Twice his father rode back to circle behind the herd, then ride up to the lead with Travis.

It must have been about three o'clock when Lance felt that the clouds were dropping lower. There was not too much wind, just fitful gusts now and then. And some of the clouds seemed to blow out of the southwest and some out of the north. The daylight turned yellowish. Beyond a crest, he and Mitch were surprised to find that his father and Travis had commenced to turn the herd in a meadow under the side of a hill. Travis signaled to them to hurry. They pushed the drag on down into the shelter of the valley.

Lance saw Juan's heavily laden wagon crawling through the grass toward a spring, and Lou Ann's wagon close behind him. A few minutes later, he saw Harden Wright ride full gallop across the meadow. Then they came on Lance's father and Travis holding a council with the rest of the trail crew. All of them watched the clouds

and tested the wind with their dampened fingers.
The spooky steer edged quietly out of the herd
and came to stand close to Lance's horse.

"Weather's not good, boys." Lance's father

said. "Think it might blow. Grab a bite to eat.
Put some sandwiches in your saddle bags. We may
be busy yet this afternoon and tonight!"

They went about their preparations quickly.

Juan was putting dry wood in the sling under the chuck wagon, which was backed, with Lou Ann's, into a kind of cave in the cliff. Then Lance noticed the pinto stamping nervously at his picket rope. Each man checked his gear carefully, saddled up, stuffed the huge sandwiches Juan handed them in their saddle bags. Each rode quickly back toward the restless herd. Lou Ann waved to him as Lance rode off. He thought she seemed frightened. He wasn't—and he was. It was funny the way the air felt and the way things looked.

He trailed Travis Cantrell and Harden Wright back, and at the bedding ground they were waiting for him.

"Lance, it's going to blow up a storm," the foreman said. He turned to look at the herd standing sullenly, watching the driving clouds. There was no wind in the meadow. "If they stampede, we'll try to turn them back into this valley. If they run, you head for the rocks. It may be pretty bad."

They rode slowly around the restless steers, trying to lull them with their songs, watching the weather, waiting. The yellow light faded. Soon it became dark, a blue darkness, Lance thought,.

and there was a kind of pressure on him as he breathed. Twice he shooed the spooky steer back into the herd as he made his rounds.

Suddenly there was a stillness Lance had never known before. A blade of grass falling down would have made a noise. It was quiet, so very quiet. Then, distantly, Lance heard a mumbling like a hive of bees swarming on a hot summer's day, but somehow different. It was like the sound of a giant musician drawing his bow on a giant bull fiddle. Lance was afraid now, and he knew it.

The sky above was suddenly blotted out by a driving rain that slashed and hurt. The rain went hurtling off across the grass and the trees, to leave a stillness that numbed the ears. Then the wind came, a wind that talked and raced madly around the sheltered valley. It tore at their clothes, pushing and pulling. Lance heard the steers bellow and tried to see them in the wind and darkness that seemed almost alive to him.

Through the surge of noise, Lance heard the steers move and knew they would stampede. He kneed the pinto forward and to the left, seeking them. Suddenly, they were running in the darkness. The little pinto plunged forward and Lance

stripped the poncho from over his head. He'd
wave it at them, try to frighten them back from
leaving the shelter of the meadow. He saw steers
beside him, wide-eyed with fear, legs churning
as they ran. Somewhere he heard a gun fired, and
another. The stampede was on!

In a blaze of lightning, Lance saw an opening
ahead in the herd and raced the pinto into it, the
poncho swinging and flaring out in the light.
They were turning back, back into the meadow!

As he made a wide turn to come back to the herd, he felt the violence of the wind tearing at his clothes. He felt the pinto stumble in mid-stride, felt himself and the horse lifted up and up. Leaves of a tree tore at his hands as he clutched at the mane of the little horse. The air was filled with the mad sound of the wind like a vast voice. Then Lance felt himself torn from the saddle and dropped down, down, down . . .

CHAPTER SEVEN

Red River Station

THE first thing Lance heard was the sound of a man groaning. He must be terribly hurt, Lance thought. Slowly, he pushed his way out of the plum thicket into which he had been dropped. His breeches were torn. There was blood on his right hand. He was dirty.

Lance crawled out of the thicket and up the slope toward the sound he had heard. He wanted to go to sleep right now, but he kept on. It was raining, a slow rain. And he could hear the wind blowing gently through the trees.

It was Travis, and he was hurt! Blood gushed all down his left arm in a big stream. His horse lay dead, all upside down against the tree above him. Lance struggled to his feet and untied the neckerchief he wore. Mother had taught him what to do. Quickly, he tied the scarf around Travis' arm, knotted the scarf, then put a stick in the slack and twisted it, round and round. The blood stopped, and he wondered what to do next.

He called and called, but no one came. His voice seemed to be swallowed up in the dense trees. Then he remembered. Travis always wore a pistol, a long-barreled Colt revolver. Lance slowly worried it out of its holster, lifted it, thumbed the hammer back. He lifted the gun and pulled the trigger. The shock almost caused him to lose hold of the stick. He thumbed the trigger back and pulled again! And again.

That was the signal for help. They might hear it. The blood had stopped spurting from Travis' arm now, but Lance remembered he was supposed to loosen the stick. He felt sick. There was the smell of the pistol smoke heavy in the trees, the quiet man, the dead horse. Where was the pinto? He didn't know. For a moment, Lance wanted to cry.

As if in a dream, the tree limbs parted, and

Lance saw John Abbott's face. He heard him call to someone, and then, his father and Ed Davis slid down beside him in the growing darkness.

"Take it easy, son." His father hugged his

shoulders. "We'll have you out of here in a minute. Travis is fine, thanks to you!"

Lance had heard about such troubles on the trails, but he had never thought he would see any of it. That was the reason for the medicine chest in Lou Ann's wagon and why his father and all the punchers knew something about doctoring men as well as cows and horses. His shoulder hurt, and there was a bruise on his right leg. But there was nothing broken for sure that he could find. Lance felt himself all over. His breeches were ripped, but he was better off than Travis just now.

He helped them lift Travis through the brush and up the slope to the horses. They rode slowly through the darkness and were careful not to let Travis slide from his saddle. Soon they could see the cook fire flickering in the night, and Lance thought he had never seen anything so friendly and so fine.

Quickly, they had Travis stretched out on his bedroll, and Juan commenced stripping the torn shirt away. Lou Ann handed Lance a big tin cup of coffee, then hurried to help Juan. Lance could smell the biting stuff in the bottle that was always used on cuts and hurts. He turned away and walked beyond the chuck wagon and crouched down in the darkness. His stomach didn't feel so good. And he was trembling all over.

"Go to sleep, son." His father spoke to him quietly. "You need it, and we'll make out for a while."

Long, long after, Lance awoke in his own bed-roll. It was dark. The fire flickered. He could make out Juan and Lou Ann. They were doctoring men by the light of a lantern. Near his head, he heard a snuffing sound. He rolled over and looked around. There stood the spooky steer and the pinto, watching the firelight and the lantern in the darkness. Lance went to sleep again.

They held the herd for two days in the little meadow by the creek. Juan filled the men full of good, hot soup, and Lou Ann was their nurse. She was a good one. The tough cow punchers did everything she said and never a word of complaint. It made Lance wonder! Those who were not hurt tended the steers. They had lost only six; the rest could move out on the Chisholm Trail.

Three, four, five days later, Travis still wore his arm in a sling. Lance had a bandage on his hand, and his shoulder hurt. They all had aches of one kind or another. Even Juan had a hurt.

He had sat down in a bed of cactus as he worked to keep his chuck wagon from blowing over! So, they moved on up the trail.

The days were filled with puffy little clouds that raced before the wind. The days were hot and the nights cool. As his hand healed, Lance enjoyed each one more and more.

"We'll make Red River Station within two days," Lance's father told him. "We pick up the last of our supplies there and cross the river into Indian Territory!"

Lance shivered at the thought. Indian Territory! Indians! He remembered Dove Song and the little warrior and the Comanches. His father had explained about it. They had to cross the big Red River, cross Indian Territory, then they would come to Kansas, then on to Abilene!

There it was! Lance didn't know what to expect. He had thought the boundary between Texas and Indian Territory might be like a high fence or a big hill or something. He saw a long, straight line on the horizon. Far beyond it the greenness of a distant riverbank faded into a far-off haze. There it was—Indian Territory.

They bedded the steers on the flat land near the river that night. As quickly as they could wash up and eat, everyone except the first night crew saddled up and rode for the big store at Red River Station. It was a low, sprawling wooden building that seemed to hold all there was in the world. Even Lou Ann, by Lance's side, gasped. They stood back as Juan and Colonel Calhoun pushed through the men in the store to reach the long counter to make their purchases.

It was noisy with the men laughing and talking. Lance bought candy for Lou Ann out of a glass jar, a whole bagful. He bought himself a new pair of leather gloves. His spurs jangled, and he felt tall enough to reach the ceiling. Just then he saw his father making his way toward the door, a loaded sack over his shoulder.

"Lance, son! Come here!" His father waited for them at the doorway, then walked with them to the horse-watering trough near the pump. "Son, you're pretty much a man now. Here's a present."

Colonel Calhoun slipped a gun belt with a holster and a bright new .44 Colt pistol down over his son's shoulder. For a minute, Lance didn't know what to do. Then he slid the gun belt off his shoulder into his hands.

"Never pull it out of the holster except when

it is needed, son!" His father looked at him, and he heard Lou Ann catch her breath. "Travis or Harden or Mitch will teach you how to use it. Let's go!"

Lance felt he would turn sidewise and upside down when he walked with the gun belt on. It was heavy. When they saddled up in the darkness, for the first time Lance felt he really was a part of the trail crew.

There had been no rain for days now. Lance thought about it for a moment. Here the river was as dry as dry where he sat the calico pony. It must be that there had been no rain way up the river valley for ever so long. There had been no talk of rain, and they had seen no clouds, nothing that could indicate the prospect of rain, for water in the Red River. Then he remembered what an old puncher had told him once.

"Never can tell, son. Might not be a cloud in a hundred or two hundred miles above us, then of a sudden down she comes rolling and tossing. Angry water, that's what it is, water gone mad. I've seen horses and cattle and men and wagons and just plain people plumb disappear in that river. And they never come back—most of them."

[*80*]

The herd was moving slowly away from the bedding ground, moving a step at a time, then a little faster, until they were strung out for nearly a mile in the direction of the fording at the river.

Lance saw a horseman riding toward the point of the herd, and he saw Harden Wright move over to talk with him. Then he saw Harden's hand lift and saw him turn his pony and race back along the rise of the moving herd.

"River's up! River's up!" Harden shouted to the herd crew. "Move out! Move 'em!" And he went racing away as they pushed the herd faster in the direction of the river.

How could it be up so quickly, Lance asked himself. Just last night, the river had been dry and there had been no water at all, just sand as far as he could see. Far ahead, beyond the trees at the riverbank, Lance could see a spume of dust lifting higher and higher into the air. He saw it whirl and tumble, higher and higher. That was the water in the river doing that. And the thought that water could make dust lift up brought a tightening to Lance's stomach. He turned a raunchy steer back into the herd with the end of his lariat, and suddenly felt afraid.

[*81*]

Lance saw Harden Wright drop his rope over the horns of the bell-cow and commence to lead her toward the riverbank, a slow step at a time. He saw men riding back and forth along the riverbank, their arms pointing, and he knew they were calling to the colonel and Ed Davis, but he could not hear what they were saying because of the bellowing of the steers and the noise of their clacking hoofs.

He could feel a change in the air. It was no longer as dry as it had been, and it smelled musty, like an old, old clothes closet that hadn't been opened in a long time. Now the steers were commencing to show signs of being afraid, tossing their horns and walling their eyes. Lance raced away to turn some of the steers back to the herd.

The bell-cow paused for a moment at the river's bank, then pushed on when Harden's rope tightened on her horns. Soon she was in the water, the steers following! Then she was swimming, muzzle up, eyes wild, but swimming, and the steers following behind her.

"It's too thick to drink, and too thin to plow!" Lance heard his father speak beside him. "We'll have trouble yet!"

Travis and Mitch and Ed Davis had ridden into the river below the swimming herd. Lance decided he had better earn his keep. He pushed the calico down the bank into the cold, tugging water. They dropped their lariats on struggling steers and helped them to the far shore. Then they returned to do it all over again with more steers. Lance was drying his face and eyes when he saw Travis' horse go down and saw Travis thrown from the saddle into the churning waters. Quickly, Lance had his lariat out and had thrown it to Travis as his arms splashed madly at the surface. In a moment, he was safe ashore and quieting his horse.

Hours must have passed, thought Lance. It was almost dark! They had to get Lou Ann's and Juan's wagons across. They were ready with big logs lashed to their undersides. Quickly the men tied their lariats to Lou Ann's wagon and fanned out with the team across the river. The wagon drifted with the current for a moment, then touched bottom, then rolled up the bank to dry ground. Lance saw Lou Ann smile with relief.

Juan was ready. They spread wide upstream for his heavy wagon, tugging against the river's

current. Just when it seemed they would make it, the wagon tipped. Its canvas cover flapped wildly, and Juan was thrown from the seat into the water. The wagon rocked on its raft of logs as Lance dropped his lariat and drove the calico madly through the water downstream. He had to save Juan!

"Juan! Juan!" Upstream, the punchers kept

their hold on the lariats, and the struggling team
touched bottom as Lance pushed after Juan. He
couldn't swim! He hadn't come to the surface
yet! Lance searched frantically. He saw a leg, then
an arm, a head. "Juan, grab hold of my stirrup!"

He saw Juan's hand reach, then slip. And the
calico stumbled and went down deep into the rolling water of the big Red River!

CHAPTER EIGHT

Monument Mountain

LANCE flung the reins out of his hand and reached for the horn of his saddle as the calico pony went down and down. As he went under, he reached for Juan, reached again and again. Then Lance's fingers clutched Juan's shirt.

As they came to the surface, Juan was beside Lance, both spluttering water and trying to breathe.

"Thank you, amigo . . ." Juan gasped. "This water is wet, and it is cold, no?"

Lance could only cling to the calico pony and to Juan's shirt as they fought their way to the far shore of the river. The calico's hoofs bit into the river bottom and heaved up through the quicksand and the mud. They were dragged to the dry bank. Juan fell on his face, and Lance fell beside him in the warm sand.

They heard horses splashing behind them, then Travis' big voice and Harden's.

"This is no time to rest, you two rascals! There's work to do and supper to cook. Move along now!"

Lance grinned to himself. As he turned he found that Juan was smiling, smiling and sick with the river water at the same time. There was work to do! And the chuck wagon? Juan looked and saw it drawn up safely on the north bank of the big river, water dripping from the raft logs, but safe! He shook his head. How could it be?

Lance shifted the heavy gun belt; the pistol was still there. Wearily, he climbed into the calico's wet saddle. This day *might* end. They had started before "can see." Now it was "can't see." As he turned the calico pony back to the crossing in the river, the last of the steers were plunging their way to the shore and up the riverbank. Lance was tired, more tired than he could ever remember.

The herd had bunched up on the slope beyond the river, their backs arched, tails stiff, their hair smelling and steaming in the cool of night. Lance wondered if every crossing of the big Red River was as bad as this one. He tried to remember if he had ever heard of a crossing here that had been easy. He swung the calico around to the horse herd and peeled the wet saddle and blanket off. He would ride the pinto tonight. Just now he wanted some food and some coffee. He was cold and wet. There were dry clothes to change into, but first came food. Before dawn had been a long time ago, and his stomach was flat.

Travis swung down by his side and spoke.

"We won't have any trouble tonight, Lance. That water took all the fight out of them and out of me, too." They walked down the little hill toward Juan's battered chuck wagon. "Old river almost bought us today, hoof, hide, and hair. That's a good river and a bad one."

There was not much talking around the cook fire that night. Lou Ann nibbled a biscuit, spoke to Lance, and climbed into her wagon. And things became quieter as they bedded down. He heard the night shift moving out in the darkness, and the next thing his father touched his shoulder. The stars told the hour of midnight as he worried sleep from his eyes. Daylight was a long way off.

By evening of the third day, they had pushed the herd up into the edge of the hills they had seen from the time they left the river. It was rolling country now, little hills, wide valleys, always climbing upward a little, and, always, there was the trace of Chisholm's Trail. The next day the trail wandered from one "best way" to another "best way," but always northward toward Abilene.

Lance had stopped counting the days. Each day was like the last. The spooky steer kept him company. Even Mitch had quit teasing him about his "watchdog steer." They drove onward, day after day, slowly, gently, from dawn to dusk.

One day Travis rode back and spoke to them. "I've told the rest of the men—this is bad country!" the foreman warned. "May be Indians from the plains; may be bad white men. Just keep your eyes open and watch!"

They did watch more than ever all the time, but there was nothing. Then there came the evening when they bedded down just below the ridge of a low hill. The evening was hazy with a kind of fog that seemed to go away when a thin slice of moon made a faint light.

As Lance rode up to the chuck wagon from the creek, he looked ahead, then looked again. He rode past the campfire and on until Lou Ann called to him:

"Lance! Here we are! Come eat your supper."

Lance stood in his stirrups and looked over the edge of the hill.

"Lou Ann! Lou Ann, come here and see this!"

Lance stepped down from the saddle, and Lou Ann walked with him toward the hill. It was a sight that made Lance think of a dream. There in the near distance seemed to stand all kinds of tall monuments, towering high above the ground, great rocks left from long, long ago. They leaned this way and that in the moonlighted night. If he didn't remember where he was, Lance thought, he might be in a cemetery. He felt a little shiver, then he heard Lou Ann.

"Oh, Lance, look! They're just like the tall headstones and cemetery monuments Aunt Caney used to tell about in her stories back home! Please, let's go back in a hurry!"

It was hours later when Lance heard the pistol shot. He scrambled out of his blankets and into his clothes and boots. Then he heard Zeke calling:

"They've got my horses! Hurry up! They've got my horses!"

Harden and Travis were ahead of him as he ran to the bushes where he had tied the little pinto. Quickly they saddled up, and as he rode away, Lance heard his father call out:

"Circle to the north! Head for Monument Mountain. They went that way . . ."

Lance followed Travis as he drove his horse through the tall grass toward the monuments that loomed in the moonlight. He saw no horses. He saw no one. Nothing! If they lost their horses, what would they do?

As they wheeled past a thicket, Lance saw something move near the towering rocks ahead of them. It was Zeke's horse herd! Travis saw it at the same instant, and so did the others who had raced to join them. They rode hard, leaning in the saddles, trying to catch up with the fleeting shadows in the moonlight. Suddenly, they were gone!

Travis pulled his horse down to a halt, lifted his hand, and stopped. He was listening. Nothing! Finally they moved on at a walk. No one knew which way to go. In the quietness, all they could hear was the light wind whispering through the tall grass.

Suddenly, as if in a wish, Lance saw the horse herd running as hard as they could go back toward them. He saw them swing to the west.

"Head them off, Harden!" Travis called as he spurred his horse. Lance was right behind him. Then Travis spoke over his shoulder. "Something turned those bronchos back to us. We'll have to find out what—"

Lance saw the vast pile of Monument Mountain loom up to the right as they raced past. It was an awesome sight in the darkness. Suddenly Travis held up his hand. The next moment, Lance heard Travis call out:

"Halt. Hands up!"

Three men sat their horses in an opening in the trees before them, hands raised. John Abbott came riding up and swung far around the men.

"Drop your guns!" Lance was surprised at the harshness in Travis' voice. "Pronto! Quickly!"

One by one, the men dropped their pistols to the ground.

"Lance! Pick them up! Put them in your saddle bags."

[*92*]

"Drop your guns!"

Lance scurried to do what Travis told him. Just then, they heard the rumble of charging horses in the distance. The next moment, Lance saw a little flag on a staff and row after row of mounted soldiers. Cavalry! They had turned the horse thieves back!

The tall figure at the head of the troop rode up to Travis, and they talked for a moment. Lance heard Travis speak his thanks, and the troop turned away with the three men in their midst.

They swung wide to bring any strays in for Zeke and found none. Then they hurried back to the campfire for something to eat. As they dropped to the ground near Juan and the big, steaming coffeepot, Lance heard Lou Ann call. The next moment, she was by his side.

"Tell me about it, Lance. Tell me!"

Lance had just started to bite a sandwich when she spoke. He told her about the wild ride after the horses and about the Army cavalry and about everything. Then he looked up to see a tall young man in uniform walking into the firelight.

"I'm Sergeant Young. The lieutenant sent me over to see if everything is all right." He looked at Lou Ann and moved to her side. "This is wild

[*94*]

country down here. We're taking the horse thieves back to the Federal Court in Van Buren, Arkansas. The Judge there will take care of them. The lieutenant just wanted to be sure you weren't having any more trouble."

Lance's father started to speak. Just then, Juan's great iron skillet rang like a church bell, a deep-throated *"brooong!"* that shook Lance inside and out, as a streak of fire fountained up into the night. A bullet had hit Juan's skillet! Lance watched the wild bouncing of the skillet as it rolled away into the darkness. Juan would be mad as hornets and honey bees all rolled into one. That was his prized skillet. He cooked everything in that skillet. Suddenly, Lance realized the noise meant someone was shooting at them.

Lance caught Lou Ann's arm and dragged her down into the shadows. He saw Juan throw a bucket of water on the fire and dive under the chuck wagon.

"The sergeant, Lance! Where is the sergeant?" Lou Ann called out. "Where is he?"

Lance wanted to crawl away from there. Sergeant! That was all Lou Ann could think about . . . that uniform! Sergeant! Another shot ripped into the faint light of the dying fire and exploded the quietness, then another, and another . . . from different sides. They were surrounded! And the herd was out there! Lance pulled the heavy pistol from its holster for the first time and commenced to crawl toward the pin oaks where he'd seen the flash of a rifle.

CHAPTER NINE

Indian Land

LANCE scrambled on his knees to the first bush. He heard Lou Ann call to him, but he went on. From the next bush was a long run to the shadows of the trees where the rifleman was hidden. Lance stumbled just as he came to the trees and fell, all the wind knocked out of him. He huddled in the darkness listening to the shots booming all around! Some came from where his father and Harden and Travis lay under the wagons. But there were more from out there and in the trees. He had to do something! Lance snaked his way through the shadows, but he could see nothing.

The noise and the smell of the smoke frightened him. He wished he had remained at the wagons. Suddenly, on the far side of the trees, he could make out a big shadow that moved. Then he could make out the long barrel of a rifle. Some-one was shooting at his father and Lou Ann and all of them!

Lance grasped the handle of the .44 pistol in both his hands and tried to sight it the way Har-den had told him. But in the dark, he could see nothing of the sight on the pistol.

As the rifle belched flame into the night, Lance pulled the trigger of his pistol and the whole grove of trees seemed to explode again and again! Lance thumbed the hammer back again and still the thundering went on. It wasn't his gun! It came from out there behind him and all around! Lance pulled the trigger again.

He heard the man in the shadow cursing, then thrashing away through the trees. There were ex-cited calls from one man to another, and the sound of horses ridden away hurriedly. It became very quiet.

"Hello the camp!" Lance spun around at the sound of the call. "We're friends! Hello the camp!"

Lance crept slowly back toward the wagons, his pistol cocked, watching for trouble. He could see the faces near the wagons raised up and watching. Out of the gloom, Lance saw the shadowy figures of six men stalking toward the camp. He suddenly recognized the sergeant! And the soldiers had their carbines ready in their hands!

"Hello, Colonel Calhoun!" All at once, the sergeant saw Lance with pistol still raised. "Don't shoot, Lance! We're friends. We came to help!"

Then Lance knew where all that shooting had come from and why the strangers had run away so suddenly. He was glad and he wasn't. The strangers were gone, but there was that sergeant again!

"Is everyone all right? Where is Miss Lou Ann?" The tall sergeant strode through the grass to the embers of the campfire. "We can put some wood on now. They're gone for good, I think."

Slowly Lance's father and the punchers climbed to their feet. His father helped Lou Ann out of the shadows.

"Whee! That was a hot surprise," said Lance's father. "Who were they? You know them, Sergeant?"

"The lieutenant sent us back on the double. One of those men you caught told him there were others in the band, and they would get even."

[99]

"Hum. Thought they wanted cattle, not us!"

"Guess they wanted both, Colonel Calhoun." The sergeant smiled at Lou Ann in the blaze of the new campfire, then turned to his men. "Ride out with the colonel's punchers and help them see that everything is all right."

As the men rode away, Lance sat down near the fire and commenced to clean his pistol. He heard his father talking behind him, then the sergeant spoke up:

"I don't think we helped as much as Lance did, Colonel. We were sneaking up when we heard that big pistol of his booming, then we started in too. They were moving by the time we got into position."

Lance ran a cloth through the barrel of his pistol, squinted at it in the firelight, then looked around. That sergeant looked mighty handsome in his uniform, and he and Lou Ann were standing mighty close. Quickly, Lance thumbed new caps on the cylinders, and pushed the pistol into its holster. He found his horse still tied behind the wagon, and mounted. Soldiers! Mother always did say a uniform could turn a woman's head!

They pushed the herd on, following the trail signs Chisholm had left to mark his trail—a great white slash in the bark of a big tree, a pile of rocks and boulders here, a pile of rocks with a pole sticking out the side and pointing, always pointing to the north along the trail he wanted them to follow. Travis had remarked that Chisholm's Trail was following the natural way along easy valleys and around the shoulders of the hills. Always, the trail avoided crossing the ravines and the gullies where a steer could fall and break a leg, or a horse might throw a rider. And it went from water to water so the trail drivers could find water for their steers. Always Chisholm's signs and markers were there just ahead of them, pointing the way and guiding them.

Day followed day without a sign of trouble. Always the spooky steer followed Lance, around the herd at night, at the tail of the drag during the day, and watching or just close by when they slept. John Abbott had long since named the steer "Rover." It was all right with Lance. He had come to like the steer with the seven-foot horns. His father didn't mind, so Lance let the steer follow him wherever he went.

They were a day short of the big Canadian
River, the herd moving slowly and smoothly along
the trail, when Lance sensed trouble.

Far ahead, in a great flat area, the herd was
being turned to bed down. There was still a good
half hour of light. As the drag of the herd moved

slowly closer, Lance and Mitch could see many men on horses. As they drew nearer, Mitch called to Lance:

"Those are Indians, Lance. They want beef, I'll bet!" They pushed on for a few minutes, then Mitch called again. "Let's get out of here! Your father may need help, and we can't help with those Indians all around us!"

Quickly, they turned and rode toward the east into the shadowy quiet of the creek. It was a swampy place, thick with tall weeds, fallen trees, and the smell of decay. It reminded Lance of a place in the valley below the ranch where he and Juan had gone one day. And he remembered the queer stump of a tree that had glowed in the twilight shadows. He shivered.

They made their way in the growing darkness until they were opposite the place where Juan had stationed the wagons. They could see the fire going and Juan hanging chunks of raw beef over the blazing coals. He was feeding the Indians!

Mitch whispered to Lance, "You wait here. I'll work around above the wagons. If they need help, maybe we can throw a rock or something!"

Mitch smiled dolefully and crawled away.

Lance stayed as long as he could stand it, then he crawled straight up from the creek to the wagons. The grass was high there, and he was hidden. He heard voices, then Harden Wright translating for his father:

"They say they want beef, sir, forty steers! They say we are crossing Indian Land, and we have to pay! And—they want the girl with the hair-on-fire!" There was a silence, then voices speaking words Lance could not understand, then Harden's voice again. "If we don't give all these to them, they say they will take them!"

Take Lou Ann? Take the steers? Lance wanted to shoot his pistol right out into the middle of them. Then he remembered there were a lot of Indians out there. And he had seen their lances, the long blades glittering in the firelight. But— Lou Ann! The soldiers and the sergeant were a long, long way away. What to do?

He didn't know where Mitch was in the dark, and it was so dark Lance didn't know where *he* was, except there were the wagons and his father and Lou Ann and the Indians. He had counted thirty of them, squat, broad of shoulder, hard-looking men. He looked again, but the darkness

was so thick he could hardly see even in the fire-light. He remembered Harden talking to him about those Indians. They were just people, Harden had said, no difference. And, Harden had said, they were afraid of things just like other people. Then Lance remembered.

Juan had run like everything that evening in the swamp, and Lance had never laughed so hard in his life.

Quickly Lance slid down to the creek's edge,
then ran back the way they had ridden. He had
tied the pinto, so he could not move. As he ran,
his eyes searched through the swampy places.
Once or twice, he kicked a stump, then went on.
Finally he came to a place and stopped. This was
it!

Lance knelt down and dug his fingers into the
glowing wood. It was like blue fire in the night!

Finally, Lance commenced to strip his clothes off, down to his underclothing. Then he pasted the glowing wood pulp on his arms and chest, made circles on his face, made lines down his legs. He heard a noise behind him and jumped around. It was the spooky steer! He walked over and tugged at the steer's horn. Within a few minutes, he had the steer plastered with the glowing material, horns, head, a long streak down his back, legs, all over. He didn't seem to mind. He just stood and snuffed at Lance.

Twice Lance debated his move. He heard the voices still talking. He could smell the meat broiling over the coals of Juan's fire. And he could see the shadow of all those Indians around the fire. They wanted Lou Ann! And they wanted the steers! Lance moved up the creek bank to Juan's wagon, then he stepped into the light and yelled that high kind of yell that made his father so unhappy. He waved his arms and jumped up and down and yelled and yelled.

For a moment, there was a complete silence, then a loud "Wagh!" Lance saw the Indians come to life like an explosion!

CHAPTER TEN

Clouds of Fire

WHAT were they going to do? Lance stopped
his dance and stood watching the Indians. They
ran every which way. When one looked at
Lance, he ran faster! Suddenly they were gone,
their horses' hoofs pounding the earth.

Lance crawled back to the creek bank and sat
down. It was a long time later when Mitch found
him, bent over his knees, sound alseep.

"Come on, Lance. They want to see you! Wake
up!" Mitch slapped him on the back and shook
his shoulder. "You scared everyone, even the
colonel, and he don't scare worth nothing! Come
on, boy!"

So Lance climbed to his feet and he was all the
way to the campfire before he remembered he had

not washed off the "fox fire." He heard a snort and remembered the spooky steer, Rover. He was still covered with the stuff too! Then he heard everyone laughing, except Lou Ann. She was crying!

"Lance! Lance! Why did you do it?" He turned, and Lou Ann had his shoulders in her hands, and the "fox fire" was all over her. "They might have killed you! You're worth a hundred steers, or a thousand, or a million!" Lou Ann hugged him tightly for a moment. "And you're all messy . . ."

Travis stood by the campfire shaking his head. Then his father came to him and led Lance away.

"That was using your head, son. A pistol wasn't enough. That 'fox fire' scared those Indians all the way back to the reservation, almost."

Two days passed and they had the herd bedded on the banks of the Canadian River. It was dry. The grass was good. A dry river, thought Lance. They wouldn't have to fight the water. Beyond the river lived Mr. Jesse Chisholm, who had marked the trail for them. They could visit him in a day or so, he and Lou Ann. He remembered the Red River, then thought about the Canadian.

They would have a good crossing. He dropped off to sleep.

Lance wondered why Travis and Harden were riding up and down the bed of the dry river. He reined in his horse and watched them in the early morning light before joining Mitch in the drag. He had seen his father holding the point of the herd back, and he wondered. A long time later, he and Mitch pushed the last of the laggards to the river's bank.

"Hold it, Lance!" John Abbott called to him. "You and Mitch follow those willow limbs stuck in the sand. It's quicky!"

"Quicky." Now what did he mean by that? Mitch pushed ahead, and Lance followed with the spooky steer, first this way, then that, across the river. Suddenly the spooky steer veered away and headed for the shore. Lance noticed that the sand where the steer ran bounced like jelly, uppy-uppy-uppy! Then the steer was down to his belly, and as he wallowed, trying to free himself, he sank deeper! He was being sucked down. Lance was frightened.

He loosened his lariat and flipped the loop far

out and down over the steer's horns, then set the calico to pulling. Mitch joined him with his rope, and they pulled together. Slowly the steer was pulled free and dragged to the hard sand on the bank.

"That was a close one for that old spooky steer!" Mitch said, dragging in his rope. "You better get smart, old steer. That'll teach you to stay away from quicksand!"

"What is it, Mitch, that quicksand?"

"Just where the water flows under the surface in the sand, is all. Can't see it until you're on it. Sometimes it just bounces 'cause there's not much water; sometimes you go *kaplump,* and there isn't any bottom to it. You get help, or you say your prayers, is all!"

They watched the steer eyeing the river angrily, and Lance laughed as they rode on after the herd.

That day and the next turned off burning hot, dry, with a strong, gusting wind whirling up out of the southwest. Every chance they had, every puncher was taking a drink of water. That night, Juan was most careful with his campfire.

"Grass is like match. No rain up here; like back there!"

Lance watched Juan and Lou Ann working at the fire with the chunks of steak. He could feel the heat, dry heat, twenty feet away. He scrubbed the dryness of his face. Tomorrow, they should be close enough to visit Mr. Chisholm.

While it was just bare daylight, they saddled up to make the trip to Jesse Chisholm's. Travis knew something of the way, so he led with Lou Ann, Lance, and his father following. They had ridden for two or three hours when they met an old Indian riding along the wagon trail.

"How!" Travis called out and raised his right hand. "Which is the way to Chisholm's place?"

The old Indian looked at them for a moment, then turned and pointed southwest.

"Go that way to Little Mountain. You find him."

"But he lives northwest from here somewhere. I know him. I've been there." Travis pointed along the trail. "Up the river."

"You go to Little Mountain. Chisholm dead!"

Dead! Lance crowded up close to Travis.

"When did he die?" Lance called out. "What happened?"

"Sick all of sudden. Die." The old Indian shrugged his shoulders. "We bury."

Slowly, they turned off in the direction of the little mountain, and later they came to a log crib around a new grave and a piece of roughly smoothed board, which read:

JESSE CHISHOLM
DIED MARCH 4, 1868.

Lou Ann and Lance gathered some wild flowers and placed them on the grave. They would never have the chance now to see the famous man. They mounted up and took the trail back to join the herd that was moving slowly and surely along the trail Chisholm had marked for them.

[*114*]

It was hot, burning hot. Lance's lips were parched. He looked at Lou Ann and handed her his canteen from his saddle bag. The herd was suffering. Now, it was worse.

Last night, Travis and his father had talked late around the cook fire. Lance had listened, storing away the stories and the remarks they had made about the dryness and heat and the risk of fire. Lance remembered seeing grass burn when he was a little boy. But that was a long time ago and it hadn't burned much. This was different. He tried to see the map his father had drawn in the dirt by the firelight. Here there were these long, long stretches of flat, grassy land and not many rivers and creeks to stop a fire if it started.

Lance told Lou Ann to wet her scarf and wipe her face, then pull it up over her nose and mouth. It might help a little as they rode on back to the wagons and the herd.

They found Juan watching the far horizon against the hot sun.

"This one hot day, amigo." Juan wiped a rivulet of sweat from his cheek. "Too hot to cook. Too hot to eat. Just too hot, me."

Lance sat down on his heels and let his body

sag in the welcome shade of the wagon. When it
was cold, he liked it hot; when it was hot, he liked
it cold. Lance smiled to himself. Time was, he
never had thought about it, but that was years
ago, it seemed.

He scrambled to his feet. He had to get back to
the herd and to work. A spinning wind-devil
passed, and the horse shied, started to break into a
run, but Lance held him down to a soft single-foot
all the way back to the herd. They mustn't spook
the steers.

By nightfall, they had the herd out of a mean-
dering creek and bedded down, but they were
restless. Travis told Lance's father he thought
they should double the night guard. All the night
long, the men riding slowly around in their turns
tried to quiet the herd and to think what the next
day might offer.

The next morning, Lance noticed the spooky
steer stayed close beside him. He turned from
time to time to look back where the wind grew
stronger and stronger. By noontime, the wind
was flattening the grass and swinging the steers'
tails. And it was so hot!

Lance had just eaten the second of the big

beef sandwiches Juan had given them when he chanced to look back again. The sky was filled with a great, dark brown cloud that moved close to the earth.

"Hey! Mitch! Look!" he called. "Storm coming!"

Mitch looked for a moment, then rode fast toward Lance.

"Go tell John Abbott to ride up and warn the colonel! That's smoke, boy, smoke! The grass is on fire!"

Lance rode as fast as he could to John Abbott, then back to Mitch.

Now they could see the angry flame leaping up in tongues of fire into the clouds of smoke, almost majestically.

"Ride up and tell your father we got to set back fires, Lance! Hurry!" Mitch swung away to pick up two lagging strays. "Go on! And hurry back!"

Lance met his father and Travis and Harden as he rode.

"Never knew it to be so dry this early!" Lance's father called to Travis. "Get that oilcan from Juan and some coals of fire. We'll need it all."

The next hour seemed to Lance to be the worst of his life. The storm cloud had come to life as they set the back fire to burn out patches of grass so the fire, when it reached there, would have nothing to feed on. As they raced along, the steers had become frightened, and the worry was that they would stampede. The drag soon left Mitch and Lance. Only the spooky steer remained behind, eyeing the fire in the grass angrily, pawing the earth as they set their own fires. Soon the air was dense with the smoke and the heat. Lance set his fires and rode on, the steer following. Soon great balloons of flame could be seen bouncing along, and the air was impossible to breathe. There was noise everywhere, and heat. They were cut off! There was fire beyond them, fountains of it, reaching to the sky! He hauled the pinto's head down and caught the steer's horns and held on. They were going to burn up!

CHAPTER ELEVEN

The Long Lances

THE spooky steer swung his rack of horns around and bellowed loud and long! Lance caught the steer's nose and pulled him close to his side. He heard the pinto whicker nervously. The grass where he had set the back fire had burned quickly, furiously. Now, it had turned black and smoky, but there was nothing more to burn. Lance dragged the pinto into the burned area and hauled the spooky steer along with one hand on the tip of a horn. They fought back at him at the edge of the burned grass, but Lance hauled them along anyway. They had to hurry! Lance was frightened. Quickly, he spread his poncho over the heads of the horse and the steer. Then he crouched down between them and held the edges of the poncho tight. It was hot and he could hear the roar of the flames now. And he felt the tug of the big wind that pushed the flames along. The wind drove ashes and bits of flaming grass and weeds under the poncho. Lance could hear the steer moan. Then the pinto swung aside nervously and squealed and tried to bolt his way out of the burned place in the grass.

Lance thought they could never live another moment. The air ceased to be air. It became a kind of heated stuff that closed in and would not let them breathe. Lance felt the pinto knee down. He caught his head and held on. Then the steer's horn pressed against his shoulder. He felt the steer tremble and stumble. Lance closed his eyes tight and wished for his father . . .

The roar was a thunder that hammered on the poncho and the heat a searing thing that cooked through the marrow inside them. Lance felt a blackness creeping up. He held to the pinto and the steer. It was so black and so hot.

How long he crouched there, Lance never knew. His first waking moment came when a breath of warm but fresh air came under the edge of the poncho. He felt the steer move, then the pinto.

Quickly he spread his poncho over the heads of the horse and the steer

Then he moved himself. The air was hot, but not so hot as it had been. They could breathe!

Lance pushed the edge of the poncho back and looked out. It was a black world. There was nothing, just acres and acres of grass burned to the roots. Some weeds still smoked. The air was filled with smoke curling down the wind that had lost some of its force.

Where was the herd? Where were his father and Travis and Mitch? Lance smelled burned hair and looked at the pinto and the steer crouched down beside him. They were burned in patches all over. He was burned! Lance felt his legs and the back of his breeches. His boots were burned.

Soon the air cleared. Lance pulled his head from under the poncho and took a deep breath of clean air. Then he heard a pistol shot and a halloo! Far across the burned area, he could see his father and Harden waving to him. He waved back, then turned to the pinto and the steer. He helped them up, petted them, rubbed their shoulders. They needed comfort. Slowly he pulled the poncho aside, folded it, and put it on the back of the saddle.

They commenced the long, difficult walk through the still smoking prairie. Finally they joined Lance's father and Travis where they waited standing on cool, unburned grass.

"Your face is dirty, Lance!" His father smiled at him. "And your two friends are just as dirty as you are!"

Lance turned and looked at the pinto and the spooky steer. They were burned and gray with ashes and trembling with weariness. He looked back at the two men.

"Your pardon, sir! You need some soap and water, too!"

Lance felt tears in his eyes. The next moment his father's arms were around his shoulders.

"You and Mitch saved us, Lance!" Colonel Calhoun patted his son's shoulder. "We tried to move around the fire, but there was a deep ravine. Your back fires stopped it just in time. We couldn't go another inch!"

They walked slowly along through the thick grass that had not been burned. Lance felt he would always remember the sound of it whispering and singing against his boots.

The herd was kept close to the bedding ground

that day and the next. They had run too far flee-
ing the prairie fire.

"They're run dry," said Lance's father. "Let
them come back to life. They're like flowers—all
of us are. Let's sit and rest."

They rested, and Lance was glad. The pinto
was tired. The spooky steer was tired.

Lance woke to a slow drizzle wetting his face at
the edge of the bedroll. It was raining! He slid
out of the blankets and worried his way into his
clothes. He was working with the straps on his
spurs, when he heard Lou Ann call.

"Lance! Lance!" She came running to him, a
poncho draped over her shoulders. "Can I ride
with you today? There won't be any dust because
of the rain. That's what you said!"

"All right, Lou Ann. All right." Lance felt
bigger somehow, because Lou Ann had asked.
She could ride with him. It was just that, the
other time, it had been dusty and no place for a
woman. "Wait until we are moving. You can find
Mitch and me."

She joined them as they pushed along through
a damp and gloomy morning. The drizzle slanted
down from time to time, then went away, to come

again. They couldn't see very far, just beyond the next turn in the trail. The spooky steer crossed behind the herd and walked up and down the herd beyond Mitch.

"Just like a bird dog," said Mitch. "He just walks up and down, up and down, smelling of the breeze. But there isn't any breeze!"

Lance thought about other times when the steer had commenced to smell around a lot.

"Lou Ann, you ride up and tell Travis and my father the spooky steer is smelling the wind. They'll know what I mean." Lance peered off through the misty distance. "Better hurry!"

"You take care, Lance." Lou Ann spoke as she rode away. "You hear me, now!"

Sounds just like Mother, Lance thought. Then he was busy and didn't have time to think. The herd dragged that day as it never had before.

Past noon, they were cresting a gentle slope. They couldn't see the top of the hill, but it didn't matter. The trail was plain to see, as wide as anyone could throw a stone. Lance fell to watching the wheel marks that must have been left by Chisholm's wagons, and the hoofs of other trail herds from the year before. As they topped the

hill, Lance saw the herd was bunched up, slowing to a stop!

Beyond the milling steers, they could see nothing. Mitch rode back and around the drag.

"I'll go see. Something has happened!" He
rode out of sight in the mist. "I'll hurry . . ."

Lance kept pushing the wandering steers back
to the slowing herd. Through the damp air, he
heard Mitch moving back. His horse was walking
slowly.

"Hey, Lance . . . Lance . . ." Mitch's voice
was swallowed up in the slanting rain. "This
way . . ."

Lance followed the voice toward the ravine to
the east. He pulled the calico up at the edge, then
moved on down.

"Lance!" Mitch's face was almost white.
"There's Indians up there—with spears!"

They'd have to see about that. Lance turned
his horse back and moved along through the rain.
Mitch followed behind him. Up ahead like a
ghost, Lance could see the spooky steer. The
steer's wide gray horns looked like wings, moving
through the rain and the fog that was beginning
to form.

[*127*]

Slowly, they moved up. Lance could make out the moving flanks of the herd. He saw John Abbott, and went on, the spooky steer always ahead. Lance saw the chuck wagon pulled up to a stop, and Lou Ann's wagon. Then he and the steer faced a line of Indians drawn up across the trail. Out of the corner of his eye, Lance could see his

father and Travis, their horses held in tight rein.

He heard the spooky steer talking in his throat, a deep, throaty rumbling that went on and on. Lance saw some of the herd steers stir restlessly and move forward a step at a time. Suddenly, there was a solid wall of steers in front of him, heads lowered. Their great horns were out and ready.

Lance saw the spooky steer look around, then swing his head. The next instant, the herd commenced to move forward. It was an angry herd, talking deep in its throat, angry and wild. Lance heard Travis call out. Then his father spoke. But there was no stopping the herd with the spooky steer in the lead.

The steer bellowed loudly, and the rest of the herd rushed after him. As they moved, the Indians plunged forward, spears raised. The next moment, Lance saw them mixed with the steers. Their horses reared up on their hind legs trying to jump over those terrible horns. Lance wanted to forget the sounds of the next moment. The horses screamed. He heard the Indians yelling. Then he heard the rising bellow of the angry steers. For an instant, in the swirling fog and rain, they were locked together. Then Lance saw a big, feathered Indian, spear lifted, riding down on him out of the mist. He tried to pull his horse back, but there was no room. He felt his horse rear up, neighing, pawing. Lance felt himself go back and down . . .

CHAPTER TWELVE

The Yellow Legs

As HE flung himself clear of the falling horse, Lance saw the spooky steer's horn slash upward. He saw the Indian thrown spinning into the midst of the bellowing steers. Then he saw the big steer, a lance buried in his shoulder, charge the Indians and their horses. Quickly, Lance dragged his horse by the reins around some bushes.

Lou Ann's wagon was there, the little team wall-eyed with fear. And she crouched behind a rear wheel, her little shotgun clutched in her hands. She was afraid. Lance dropped beside her. He peered out through the wheel spokes just as a pistol boomed into the closeness of the thick fog. Then another! Each hammering sound seemed to stop the mad noise of the angry steers and the frightened horses.

Suddenly, it was quiet. The Indians had gone! Lance pushed Lou Ann back and scrambled out to his horse. Beyond the chuck wagon and the bushes, Lance could see the great ring of steers. They watched the direction in which the Indians had gone. They were still angry. Lance could hear the sounds they made in their throats and see them shaking their horns. An Indian pony lay dead in the opening. Tasseled lances stuck at angles in some of the steers. Beyond the dead pony, a steer coughed, fell to his knees, then rolled over dead!

Lance went to find his father or Travis or anyone behind the steers. He was surprised, as he moved along, to find the whole herd standing so tense. Why didn't they stampede? Beyond the herd, he found Harden with his carbine across the horn of his saddle, watching.

Harden whistled softly, and Lance heard his father call back. In a moment, he and Travis and John Abbott had joined them.

"Did you ever see anything like those steers? But those Indians may come back. This isn't good!" Colonel Calhoun sat quietly for a moment. "What do you think, Harden?"

"Don't know, Colonel. If those steers had faced me that way, I'd still be running. But those were Cheyennes, and they are tough warriors. I think maybe they'll be back in two or three days."

Later the fog lifted a little, and the herd was moved on to a wide valley beyond the hill. There they made camp. By good nightfall, the wind had risen. The fog began to move away, little by little. Soon they could see the stars overhead and the glow of a moon commencing to rise in the east.

They had finished their beans and beef when a voice hailed them from the creek below.

"Halloo, the drive. Colonel . . . Calhoun! Friend . . . Friend!"

Travis answered, and they saw a horse and rider loom out of the distant shadows. The stranger held his hand lifted as he rode toward them in the half-light.

"Colonel Calhoun?" Lance's father came forward. "A lieutenant and a sergeant of dragoons told me to find you. A bunch of renegade whites plan on taking your cattle. They're twice as many as you!"

"Step down, man. Meat and beans and corn-bread. Welcome." Colonel Calhoun motioned to Juan. Lance watched the tall man dismount. "You mean that bunch from way south we had trouble with at the Monuments?"

"Lieutenant said they slipped out of his trap, and for me to ride this way and warn you. I'm on my way to the Rockies. I'm Peter Claibourne. My pack train is down in the creek bottom."

"Indians! And now those rascals again—" Colonel Calhoun motioned to Travis and Harden, then walked with them beyond the firelight.

"The Indian country is full of bad whites, Colonel," Peter Claibourne said. "They're every-where from Fort Smith to the high plains. That's why I've been sticking to the low places and mov-ing mighty quiet."

"Has there been much trouble with herds?"

"Wasn't last year." Peter Claibourne answered. "This year the bunches have more men, so they shoot first and steal later. They rob everyone, whites and Indians alike."

Lance remembered how it had been for a while after the Civil War. Twice men had come to the ranch before his father had finally come home.

They were a mean lot with dirty clothes and scraggly beards. But the big house was like a fort and the family had stayed inside until the men went away. Now, it was different. Lance thought of the cattle herd and all it meant, their supplies in the chuck wagon, and Lou Ann! The renegades would hurt Lou Ann, and that was worst of all.

He heard his father speak suddenly and turn back to the fire.

"We need help from somewhere. We can't stand that many off. There's nothing behind us for days since that high water cut them off at the Red River."

The three men sat drinking Juan's coffee and talking quietly or just thinking out loud. There had to be an answer somewhere. Lance checked his guns and wondered what to do.

He found his weary way into his bedroll near Juan's chuck wagon. He heard Lou Ann talking with Juan. He slept. But it was only for a moment, it seemed. He felt his father touch his shoulder and whisper to him. Lance pushed the blankets back.

"Son, come along. We need you!"

Fully dressed, Lance made his way to the firelight. The stars had swung far to the west. Must be nearly midnight. Lance crouched down near his father and Harden.

"Son, we're headed for trouble. Harden says those Cheyennes will come back. Mr. Claibourne says those men are out to steal the first herd over the trail. We need help." Colonel Calhoun smoothed a place on the ground in the firelight. "Here we are. North of us is a trail headed west. General Custer has occupied one of the temporary posts the Army has set up about two hours to the west of a point about here." Colonel Calhoun made a mark on the map on the ground. "If you head northwest you can cut a trail that leads to the post in about one hour. You're the lightest. Will you take Lou Ann's Barb mare? She's the only horse we've got that's built for long running. Our horses are all working horses. Take the Barb and ride northwest until you cut that trail. Find Custer and ask for some cavalry. You can find the post before morning. Leave your carbine. Take your hand gun."

The spooky steer stood behind Juan's wagon as Lance saddled Lou Ann's little mare. He watched as Lance slipped quietly away in the night. After the first half hour, Lance pushed the little mare out into a long, trail-eating lope. Then he walked, loped, walked. He cut the west trail only when the mare snorted and pulled up for a minute. Otherwise, he might have

missed it. Twice, he stepped down to walk a little, to breathe the mare, and to swab the dust from her nostrils. He pushed on. And finally, in full starlight, he made out the ragged outline of a pole stockade near a dry river. Then he heard a guard challenge near the gate when he slid to the ground in the darkness.

In a moment, Lance had been conducted to a tent. That was about all he saw, tents evenly spaced here and there over the area. A few moments later, a bright-eyed man with yellow hair and a yellow mustache came into the lantern light. It took but a moment for Lance to tell his story.

"Cheyennes and renegade whites!" the officer whispered. He barked for a sergeant. A corporal handed Lance a huge sandwich and a cup of tea, then pushed him toward the door. A soldier was rubbing down the little Barb mare, cleaning her nostrils, letting her drink sparingly. Lance heard a bugle sound and watched a small troop of cavalry with yellow stripes down their legs mount up.

"They're waiting for you, son!" The corporal took the empty tea mug. "That little mare of yours can go twice as far! Wish we had a hundred like her! Good luck. Hurry along!"

Lance rode beside the lieutenant commanding the little troop. From time to time he dozed in the saddle. He heard the scout's hail when they found his marks entering the trail, then pushed on. The troop was moving fast. The little mare swung into a long lope, breathing easily, enjoying the run. Finally, Lance spoke up.

"Lieutenant, the trail must be beyond the ridge there. If the herd hasn't passed, we can cut around it and drop back."

"Good thinking, young fellow." The lieutenant lifted his gloved hand. Short of the hill, they stopped for a moment for word from the scout. He waved them on, but the lieutenant signaled him back. "Let's stay back of this ridge and use this early morning light. If there are Indians, they're behind us. If there are those bad whites, they won't see us. Let's keep under cover."

The scout signaled to them, and the lieutenant moved to the ridge. A moment later, he motioned to Lance.

"Are those the white men who attacked you?" He motioned beyond the winding valley. Lance looked. The lieutenant handed him a pair of field glasses. Lance found them, studied for a minute. "Do you recognize any of them?"

"Yes, sir! He was just a shadow, but that big man with the rifle in his hand is one of them!"

The troop moved quietly below the ridge until they came to a ravine covered with trees and bushes. They threaded their way through it until they came to a plum thicket. Suddenly, they saw the point of the herd, Lance's father and Travis far out, the two wagons behind them, then the herd.

Just then the renegade whites broke from the cover of the valley beyond. The riders spread out in a fan to take in Lance's father and Travis, the wagons, and the point of the herd. Lance saw the lieutenant lift his hand, heard the bugler's shrill charge, as the troop pushed out of their hiding.

For an instant, Lance rode with them, then he turned the plunging little Barb mare toward the wagons. Someone had to look after Lou Ann and Juan. He pulled his pistol and thumbed the hammer back as he rode close to Lou Ann's wagon. He reached for the brake rod, and swung up from the little mare's saddle. Then he turned the wagon to the left as he saw the troopers and the renegades come together. The herd followed the wagon.

[*140*]

CHAPTER THIRTEEN

Arkansas Crossing

LANCE heard the bugle sound off loud and clear, just as Lou Ann caught his shoulder. Her little mare paced excitedly beside the wagon. Then Lance stared, amazed. The spooky steer ran quietly behind the mare. The steer's head was swinging from side to side, watching. Lance heard him bellow.

As the herd turned, Lance looked back. Juan had his wagon following. Soon they came into the shelter of a high bank of earth where a spring gushed from a ledge of rock. Lance handed the driving lines to Lou Ann and climbed down. The little mare was about spent, but she would have to do until he found Zeke and one of his mounts. He heard the firing drawing away from the north

[*141*]

and the sound of men calling. Lance made his way on around the herd. He'd bunch them, then join his father and the troopers! As he rode, the spooky steer trotted behind.

He came on John Abbott and Ed Davis on the far side near the creek. They were listening to the firing.

"They're moving!" Ed said. "Those soldiers got that gang on the run . . ."

Lance rode on, and John Abbott came with him. They stopped where the herd had commenced to mill. Soon his father and Travis came back to join them. Then Harden rode back, blood smearing his left arm.

"Soldiers shot three of those men up there. We'll have to bury them—and maybe others." He sagged in the saddle. Lance caught him as he slid down. "I'm all right. Just tired."

They brought Lou Ann's wagon over and put Harden on the camp bed. Then she and Juan went to work on Harden's arm. Later, Juan climbed down and set to cooking at his fire.

"He be all right, that Harden. Indian tough man." Juan spread huge cuts of beef on the racks over the coals. "Those soldiers, they be hungry."

He nodded his head and smiled. "Beans, beef, and *bisquit,* you bet!"

As darkness fell, the troop came riding up to the camp. Lance's father talked with them, then they made camp by the edge of the creek, quietly and orderly. Lance watched them in the twilight. Those uniforms *were* handsome!

All that night, they were paired with armed soldiers as they watched the herd. The steers were tired. They paid no attention to the scent of strange men. When the moon came up, they paid no attention to the sight of the uniforms and carbines.

During the night, Travis and the lieutenant had supervised the burying of the dead bandits beside the creek. In the morning, the herd moved on with the troop of soldiers riding as flankers and scouts to the east and the west. They would ride with them all the way into Kansas. The Indians might come back, or maybe the bad men.

"This is wild country," said the lieutenant and shook his head.

The lieutenant told Lou Ann and Lance about his duty there in the plains country. And he told them about the long string of army posts that extended all the way from Nebraska, across Kansas and Indian Territory, deep into Texas. Some were made of stone and were good to live in. But there were others that were just mud and sticks, and some just dug out of dirt walls and called dug-outs. And all of this was to keep watch over the Plains Indians and prevent them from raiding the settlements.

Now these bands of bad white men were causing as much trouble as the Indians, almost. Lance thought how grim it was to have enemies on both sides. Then he was glad someone had thought to put the soldiers out here on the prairies to watch over things. He remembered the stories told around the fireplace at home, about how the wily Comanches came raiding down into Texas in the full of the moon. He remembered the old, old man who had come to the ranch one day, a twinkle in his blue eyes, but no hair on his head. He'd been scalped and left to die, but he lived somehow to reach Fort Griffin. And they had captured women and children to hold for ransom. He thought of Lou Ann and shuddered.

Suddenly, he was glad the Army was with them, and he wanted to tell the lieutenant, but he was a little shy and said nothing. He would thank him some other way, some time.

In the days that followed, the soldier scouts twice reported Indians riding far to the west. But they did not come close. Lance breathed a sigh of relief. He had worried about Lou Ann. She had nursed Harden Wright tirelessly. Now he was taking day herd with the rest of them and wearing his arm in a sling.

They had climbed out of the "red" soil of Indian Land and had come to the flat-as-the-eye-could-see grassland of Kansas. The soldiers rode with them, glad for the break in their duties. And at night, they enjoyed Juan's cooking, beans and whatever else, but always beans.

One day away from the Arkansas River, the herd was hit by a wild prairie storm that was gone as quickly as it had blown up. They watched the purple and blue cloud with its train of rain drive northeastward across the prairie. That night the sky to the north was a solid blanket of clouds filled with lightning.

Lance's father and Travis sat by him and watched.

"That means the flat land west of the Arkansas

[145]

will be covered with water." Colonel Calhoun scratched a map on the ground in the firelight. "We'll have to cross here to the high ground and head on up the river to Chisholm's Ranch on Chisholm Creek. That's seven or eight miles above where he took those Wichita Indians during the war."

"What did Mr. Chisholm have to do with the Wichita Indians during the war?" Lance asked his father. "You mean he moved the whole tribe by himself?"

"No, he didn't pick them up and carry them." Colonel Calhoun smiled at Lance. "But he did lead them all the way up here from across the Red River in Texas. Some of the Indian tribes took sides with the North and some took sides with the South in the Civil War. The Wichita Indians were Union sympathizers, and they were afraid of what other tribes might do to them if they stayed down in Texas. So they asked Jesse Chisholm to find them a new place to live and to take them to it. He was always doing good things for the Indian tribes in Indian Territory. He traded with them. Brought them the things they needed. He met with the government agents when they came out from Washington and helped the tribes make treaties, and he gave them good advice. When the time came for the Wichita Indians to move northward to safety, Jesse Chisholm knew just the place to take them."

Colonel Calhoun drew a circle on his map in the dirt where two rivers came together. Then he stuck a little stick in the middle of the circle.

"Right here is where the Big Arkansas River and the Little Arkansas River come together. Right here is where Jesse Chisholm had made a ranch." The colonel pointed to a spot northeast of the place where the rivers came together. "He knew the grass was good; there was plenty of water and wood; there is a lot of game all through here, so he brought the Wichita Indians across Indian Territory over the trail we have followed. There were a lot of them. Then, when the Civil War was over, they went back south. The soldiers who helped us against those thieves told me a land company is going to build a town right there where the rivers come together. We'll move the herd along the high ground to the east of the place where the rivers join. There'll be good water and grass at Chisholm's Ranch."

[*147*]

By midmorning the next day, the herd had moved in to where the ground was soggy from the rain the night before. The clouds still hung off to the north, black and threatening. By noon, under a bank of clouds that were commencing to spit rain, they reached the Arkansas River.

The soldiers grouped up just long enough for the lieutenant to shake hands with Lance's father, formed up, and headed back to the southwest. Lance watched the double column from the drag and waved to them.

Travis had taken the point of the herd down into the half-dry river by the time Lance shrugged his scorched and burned poncho down over his head. It was beginning to rain heavily and to blow in wild gusts. The wagons had crossed and had made the higher ground to the northeast when Fitz Land and John Abbott worked the flanks of the herd down into the river.

They rode back to give Mitch and Lance some help. As the herd poured down over the riverbank, they worked as flankers, hunched over against the rain and the driving wind. The spooky steer trotted close beside Lance, eagerly watching the riverbank. He was thirsty, and here was water! Lance turned back, rounded up a stray, and pushed to the bank. Just as the pinto dropped over the bank to the river, Lance looked to the north.

His heart climbed into his mouth, and he struggled to yell above the noise of the moving steers. The river was boiling from bank to bank with live, rushing water, a mile above them! Cloudburst! Fitz saw Lance pointing, and so did Mitch and John Abbott. They swung their ropes' ends and yelled to move the steers out of the river.

The steers sensed the danger and commenced to crowd the far riverbank. Lance rode frantically with Fitz and Mitch close by his side. The steers fought to move out of the river bottom. They could hear the noise of the water now, a low rumble. Then it was upon them!

Lance saw the water surge into the drag of the herd, then fountain up over them, burying them. The steers fought back, lunging, bellowing, swimming. He saw Fitz's horse pushed down under the water, and he saw Fitz struggling for the shore.

Then Lance's pinto went down with a frightened whicker. The spooky steer was right beside

[*149*]

him when Lance came to the surface in the mad water. He fought the poncho for an instant, and one hand caught the steer's outstretched tail.

Lance clung desperately and tried to swim as much as he could. A drowning steer's horn grazed his side, but he caught his breath and held on, trying to make the shore that seemed so close, yet so very far away.

CHAPTER FOURTEEN

Iron Wire and Fence Posts

LANCE'S hand slipped from the spooky steer's tail. He felt himself rolled under in the water. A ragged tree limb caught him and held him for a moment. His breath was gone. He fought feebly with his arms. His hand touched the dragging limb of a willow. He caught hold with all his strength and held on. The pressure of the water lifted him to the surface, and he could breathe fresh air.

Above and below him, he could see the steers clambering up the bank. The pinto floundered and went under. He saw John Abbott and called with all his voice. He was calling again when the limb broke, and he dropped beneath the rushing water. A moment later, Lance fought to the surface again and heard a loud voice.

"Grab it, Lance. The rope—the rope!" It was John.

A moment later, Lance slipped the lariat down over his shoulders and was hauled ashore. He lay spitting out water, until John Abbott slid down to him in the mud.

"That was a close one, Lance! You all right?"

John Abbott helped him up, and they crawled up the riverbank to the steers. They looked for the other punchers. There was Mitch Tally. But where was Fitz Land? And where was the spooky steer?

They rode the bank of the river until dark, all of them. But they could not find Fitz. They found his horse, but they could not find Fitz. Night came on, and the weary trail crew gathered around the fire Juan had built. There was food, but no one wanted to eat. Even the herd of steers stood looking back at the river that had been so false to them. Lance went back to his daily work with the tally book. That book had to be right. His father had told him that.

When he had finished, Lance took Fitz's saddle and put it on the calico. Then he rode the riverbank for miles trying to find Fitz and the pinto and the spooky steer. It was midnight when his father caught up with him.

"Son, it's rough on you. I know. Trail herding has always been one of the most dangerous jobs on earth." They rode silently for a few minutes. "Sometimes we have warning. Mostly we don't. Maybe it is better that way. Let's go back."

Except for a small guard, the entire crew spent the next day riding the riverbank. The water had gone down now, though it still rained. Late in the afternoon, when the sun was slanting low, they found the spooky steer on a sand bar. It appeared to have tried to crawl out. Then they found Fitz Land. The pinto munched grass and watched near by.

It was open country, so they dug a grave on the high ridge back from the river. Lou Ann and all the crew were there. Lance's father said a few words, then they shoveled in the earth. They made a high mound and placed pieces of limestone on the mound. If Fitz could see, he could look back the way he had come over the Chisholm Trail.

Lance went to look at the spooky steer once more, then turned away. Come tomorrow morning, they had to be on their way up the trail to Abilene.

Two days later, at nightfall, they bedded the herd at Chisholm's Ranch. Rain had fallen all the time. So they followed the high ground, winding this way and that. Always they had stayed in sight of the river until they reached the high ground east of the Little Arkansas River. Then they had swung northeast.

Here was a good place to rest and to repair their gear. Except for his town clothes, Lance felt he must look like a scarecrow. Juan broke out his bootmaker's equipment and put new heels on all their boots. Then Lou Ann set to work with her needles and thread mending jeans and shirts. Their supplies were holding up, but Juan would have to stretch some things. Lance laughed to himself. The little sugar they had when they started up the trail had long since gone. But the molasses was holding out and that was good for everything from cornbread and biscuits to sweetening coffee in the morning. There wasn't any dried fruit, but they would reach the end of the trail soon and then they could have anything they wanted. More than anything, Lance thought, he and Lou Ann would like some stick candy, the kind with stripes all down the sides. Better not tell Travis.

They mended harness and saddles the second day and even put a new tongue on the chuck wagon. It was good to sit under the big canvas sheet stretched over poles and rope and listen to the rain pittering down. Even duty with the herd was not hard. The steers seemed to want to rest, too. But Lance missed the spooky steer and sometimes felt that if he turned quickly enough he would see him walking right behind him as he made his rounds.

The rain let up, though the clouds remained. There was dry wood in a shed, and there was water. The herd found good grass. The Calhoun trail herd rested. Later, Lance sat with Lou Ann to work on his tally book in the light of Lou Ann's lantern. They heard a rider.

"Halloo the camp! Friend . . . this is a friend . . ."

Into the light of the campfire where the crew sat or lay or slept, a man rode.

"My name is Herrington. I'm a cattle buyer." He climbed down from his horse. Lance's father stood up. "Want to do business?"

Colonel Calhoun looked at him for a minute.

"Can't, Mr. Herrington. I made a contract with McCoy a year ago."

Herrington, his sparse, thin body stretched to its tallest, spoke:

"That was a year ago. This is now! I've got money, good money!" His voice became excited. "That McCoy, what do you know about him? He'll cheat you. I'll give you good money right now!"

"He's a gentleman, for one thing!" Lance's father spoke slowly and carefully. "And money or no money, I gave him my word I'd deliver cattle. These are his cattle. Go back where you came from!"

The little man hesitated in the shadows beyond the fire.

"All right, but you watch out. You're going to

have trouble with the farmers. I'll see to that. You wait!"

Lance thought about the stranger's remarks as he dropped off to sleep. He was thinking about it on night herd, and the next morning as he rode along. The farmers!

The first day above Chisholm's Ranch, no one bothered them. The trail was plain. The second morning a Texas puncher cut their trail and rode in to talk. Mitch sent him up to the point to find Lance's father. But there were no farmers that day, or the next, or the next. They circled slightly to the east of a small village, and gradually back to due north by the north star.

That night, all of the crew not on night herd held a council of war. Lance's father told them the puncher had reported that the farmers ahead of them were up in arms. They did not want their fields trampled down. And they were afraid of tick fever from the steers.

"We won't go near their fields. And I've seen no tick fever in these steers of ours." The colonel paused for a moment. "That puncher said a little man was rousing the farmers up. He wanted the first Texas herd over the Chisholm Trail!"

They pushed on the next morning. The day had dawned bright and clear. It would be a warm day, so Mitch said. They pushed on along until long past the noontime. As the drag of the herd dropped over a small hill into a valley where a creek wound round, he could see the point far ahead. But the point had stopped! He could see men up there, some on foot, some on big horses.

As they pushed through the creek, Lance could see Travis and John Abbott turning the point and swing of the herd back on them. He saw his father motion with his arm westward, and Harden Wright and Travis swung the point to the west without stopping.

As the herd snaked its way up the slope of the hill, Lance watched as best he could. He could make out something that looked like a fence, but with no rails. Then he saw smoke bloom from a gun, then again, and again!

By this time, the herd had commenced to run. The flanking punchers tried to slow the herd down. They rode in and out, but the herd gradually moved faster until they were in full trot. Stampede, this was a stampede for sure, thought Lance! They wouldn't be able to stop it! He saw the herd commence to turn back toward the north. But they were moving faster! What could they do? The steers were bunching, bumping into each other.

Lance pulled the pinto around and rode hard for the north flank of the herd. The next thing, he was close to a long row of posts in the ground with iron wire strung from post to post. He had never seen anything like it. He found Ed Davis and John Abbott riding the bunched flank of the herd.

"Fence ends up there, Lance! But they've got shotguns! They've stopped us!" John rode beside him. "They're talking mighty mean!"

Lance saw his father sitting his horse in front of a solid line of steers. Their heads were lowered, and they were commencing to stir angrily. Then two men rode out on big harness horses. One man had a gun.

"You turn around and go back! You hear!"

Lance's father looked at the man for a moment.

"We won't touch your farms, and we won't touch your fences. We won't go back!"

Lance saw the farmer's gun lift toward his father's head, and saw the gun bellow gray smoke

One man had a gun

twice. The noise shocked everything quiet for an instant. Without thinking, Lance's lariat shot out and wrapped itself around the farmer's gun barrel and jerked. The next instant the farmers charged. Lance heard his father calling just as a big horse rode over the pinto and Lance went down!

CHAPTER FIFTEEN

Trail's End

LANCE rolled clear of the pinto's flailing hoofs. The next instant, the pony fought back at the big farm horse. Lance heard the horse squeal and saw the farmer thrown head over heels! There were the sounds of two more shots, then sudden silence.

"Stop this!" The voice cut through everything. "Stop it!"

Lance peered out and up through the horses' legs. A medium-sized man sat a sorrel saddle mare. He had his hand raised. Gradually, the clashing forces moved apart.

"My name is McCoy! I'm a cattle buyer in Abilene. I bought these cattle a year ago. These are my friends!" The voice paused for a minute.

"Let's stop this. This herd must move on . . ."

By the time Lance had climbed back into the pinto's saddle, Travis had the herd moving. Colonel Calhoun sat his horse beside the man and talked. The farmers moved slowly back. Lance looked at the fence with its row of posts and that funny stuff they called wire nailed to them. He breathed a sigh of relief. Maybe, just maybe, they would reach Abilene.

They moved slowly. Five days later, they came over the crest of a low hill and saw a broad grassland below. Far beyond, Lance saw his father and Travis turning the point of the herd. Juan's wagon and Lou Ann's had pulled off to one side. He and Mitch moved up gently to push the drag down for the last time. They moved slowly and surely, a task that was old now, but one that had to be done right this last time.

As the big herd slowly circled back on itself, Lance could not help feeling proud. The steers were sleek and fat and so trail-wise it took only a little while to have them bedded down for the night. For a moment, Lance wondered about putting them into loading pens. They had never seen anything like that and it might cause trouble. But he knew that his father and Travis had given it thought and probably had an answer.

The grass was good here, and there was a stream for water. Lance sat his horse for a little while just watching the herd, then turned to look toward where Abilene was supposed to be. They'd be there tomorrow. Then Lou Ann would go on to St. Louis.

Lance felt a small ache inside and knew he would miss her when she was gone. She had come all the way up the trail with them, through everything the trail had to offer, and never once cried. Lance shook his head. Girls could be just as strong as men when they had to be. Lou Ann had been. He wished she was going back to Texas with them, back to the ranch to stay.

Suddenly, he turned his horse and raced back toward the chuck wagon. There were clothes to see about, and Lou Ann needed some help with her packing. There was a lot to do.

Tomorrow, in the morning, the herd would be driven into Mr. McCoy's new loading pens by the railroad. Lance rolled the word on his tongue—railroad! Far ahead, he saw a plume of smoke fountain up, but it was too far to see for certain.

Lance checked his tally book for the last time that evening by Juan's fire. The herd had started with eleven hundred steers. Two legs broken the night the wind walked; three lost at the big Red River; two lost when the Cheyennes came; nineteen lost when the flash flood caught them at the Arkansas River. Lance drew a line. He added it up. Twenty-four lost. And one was the spooky steer. The cattle business was a hard job. Lance climbed to his feet to find his father and give him the tally book.

The last steer was in the new loading pens by high noon. For the last half hour, Lou Ann and Lance had been perched on the corral rails nearest the railroad tracks. Half the time, Lance had been watching the big engine that puffed so much smoke and grumbled inside and leaked steam. Down the rail from them, a man in a storemade suit and a round-topped hat had put a foot on a bottom rail. He watched with them for a while. He had said nothing, but only watched and made notes in a little notebook. Finally Lance's father found them.

"All through, Lance? Your tally was right." Lance's father leaned against the rail and wiped his face with a handkerchief. "Wish Fitz was with me. And that spooky steer. We'd have had to take the steer home. He was one of the family." Colonel Calhoun turned and called to them, "Let's go. We sleep in beds tonight!"

As they walked away from the loading pens, the stranger in the round hat came up to them.

"Pardon, what kind of cows are those?" The stranger asked. "My name is Morris, William Morris. I'm from Boston, back East. I write for magazines and newspapers."

"Those are Texas Longhorn steers, sir! In six months or a year, those steers will be meat on your table in Boston!" The colonel paused. "Forgive me. I'm Bruce Calhoun. Join us for lunch at the hotel. Mr. McCoy would like to have you."

"I've known McCoy for some time. I'll lunch with you, surely. He told me you were on the way. That's why I'm here! The first herd over the Trail in 1868—that is news!"

They trudged on to the rail tracks and crossed them. Then they walked down the long, dusty street on a walk made of boards.

"Father!" Lance caught the colonel's arm. "I don't want to go back yet. I want to go on with Lou Ann and get some schooling in St. Louis. I know for sure now that what I want to do is raise

cattle, and that takes learning, I guess." They walked on a short way. "I could look after Lou

Ann and maybe learn something to make the ranch bigger when I come back."

"That's fine, son, fine." Colonel Calhoun smiled. "That's thinking like a man!"

Mr. Morris was talking with Lou Ann as they walked along the boardwalk under the shade of the wooden awnings. Finally they came to the steps of the hotel. Lance looked around the street and at the long row of stores and offices. The street was filled with wagons and buggies and saddle horses. There were more people than he had ever seen, even in San Antonio. Behind the big buildings, he could hear the chuffing of the rail engine that would carry the steers away east. And now he would go, too.

He and Lou Ann looked over the great lobby of the hotel before walking in. There were chairs everywhere, and a big counter, and chandelier lights in the ceiling. And there was a wide stairway, a big one! An old man took Lou Ann's big case and her hatbox. Then he picked up Lance's bedroll.

"This way, please!"

He led them up the stairs and down a hallway. At one door, he stopped.

"This is yours, young sir."

Lance saw him open the next door and put Lou Ann's case down.

"Colonel Calhoun and Mr. McCoy and Mr. Morris are on both sides of you. Here's your key."

After a hot bath, Lance slept for what seemed to be hours. He woke to find Harden and Mitch leaning over his bed and laughing.

"We hit the end of the trail in Abilene and you go to sleep!" Mitch grinned. "Me, I been watching that big wood-eating engine that's taking our steers away."

"What you been doing, Harden?" Lance asked as he rolled off the bed to find his clean clothes. "I asked if I could go to St. Louis to school. I'm going to school. I really am."

"Well, Lance," Harden said, "I'm going back and marry Miss Dove Song! That's her name because she is Cherokee Indian. Her American name is Lenora Wright. And we're going to ranch back home!"

Lance shook his head and dressed. A tap on Lou Ann's door, and she joined them in the hallway, all fluffy in a white dress and stockings and shoes that shined.

[*171*]

"Lou Ann." Lance handed a flat package to her. "Here is something I bought for you way back down the Chisholm Trail in San Antonio. It was supposed to be a kind of good-by."

"Oh, Lance!" She pulled at the knot in the leather string and slipped off the paper. "Oh, such a beautiful comb! Just like the ones all the señoritas wear. And for me! Thank you." Lou Ann turned back to her room. "I'm going to wear it tonight. Wait a minute."

Her eyes were bright as they went to his father's door.

"Lance, I'm going to miss you!" she said.

"No, you're not. Because I asked Dad, and he says I can go to St. Louis with you!" Lance announced triumphantly. "I want to go to school— and learn something—"

"Well, I declare, Mr. Lance Calhoun!"

Behind them, they heard Colonel Calhoun and Mr. Morris from Boston laughing. All the way down to the dining room, Lance and Lou Ann were very quiet. As they stepped through the door, Lou Ann gasped.

"Everyone is here, every last one! There's Juan."

Lou Ann turned around excitedly. "There's that Mr. McCoy!"

Soon they were all seated around a long, long table with a white cloth and dishes and silver. It was pretty and clean. And the lamps on chains made a pretty light. The waiters moved around busily. Then Mr. McCoy stood up. He smiled at all of them.

"This is a dinner for all of you, for all of you here, and for one who did not reach Abilene. Mr. Chisholm marked the trail. You made the Chisholm Trail. It has been a long journey. Tonight, some of the steers you drove will be shipped to the East. I am proud. I thank you."

The man from Boston was writing in his little book. He leaned over to speak to Colonel Calhoun, then the two of them rose from their chairs. Colonel Calhoun spoke to Lance.

"Son," he said, "if you want to travel with Lou Ann to St. Louis, we'll have to be going. We'll put the little mare in the baggage car. You can ride along and look after her."

When they left the hotel the next morning, Lance wore his new black suit, his new puncher's

[*173*]

boots, and the new broad-brimmed hat his father had given him. They had kept Lou Ann's little mare in the stable near the hotel. Lance was to walk the little mare to the railroad yard while his

father took Lou Ann and their parcels and suit-boxes.

Wagons filled the long streets as Lance threaded his way toward the station. He listened to the sound of men and children laughing and talking. They hadn't heard much like that for a long time. At the station, the agent came to show Lance how to put the little mare on the platform so she could enter the baggage car. She stepped nicely and daintily, ears pricked, eyes watchful, but she moved right along. Lance was proud of her. The baggage clerk helped him open the stall gate, and Tina walked right in and turned around to watch. They felt the car tremble, then begin to move.

Tina nuzzled Lance's shoulder as he leaned out to look back and wave. Lou Ann and Mr. Morris were watching him from the platform of the coach behind. And on the station walk, Lance could see his father and all the punchers waving to him.

Already the hot sun was shining, and the south wind was whipping up the dust of Abilene town as they pulled away from the station. Far to the south, Lance could see dust on the Chisholm Trail. His adventure was over, he realized a little sadly, but he'd be back!

About the Author

ROSS MCLAURY TAYLOR is a fourth generation Southwesterner, from Virginia, Tennessee, and Georgia, by way of Texas. He graduated from the University of Oklahoma, did post graduate work at Harvard under such eminent educators as Dr. George Lyman Kittredge, and received his doctorate at the State University of Iowa. A rated airplane pilot, he has also been a cow puncher, boxer, and polo player. He served as a lieutenant colonel in Military Intelligence during World War II and in the Korean War. A writer of historical fiction, text books, articles, short stories, and critical reviews, his primary interest, besides hunting, fishing, flying, and photography, is Southwestern Americana.

About the Artist

CHARLES BANKS WILSON, well known to young people for his illustrations of many historical books about the West, has achieved equal success as a painter. Over 150 exhibitions of his works have been held in museums throughout America. In both book illustration and painting, Mr. Wilson is associated with the contemporary life of the American Indian. Many Indian ceremonials which have never been photographed are recorded in his work, which has taken him throughout the Southwest as well as the Far West. He lives in his native Oklahoma, with his wife, a Quapaw Indian princess, and their two children. Since 1947, he has been head of the Art Department of the Northeastern Oklahoma A. & M. College.

About the Historical Consultant

STANLEY VESTAL was born on a claim near the Flint Hills in Kansas, and came to the Oklahoma Territory as a boy. He graduated from Southwestern State College in 1908, and from Oxford University in 1911, as the first Rhodes Scholar from the new state of Oklahoma. Since then he has been a teacher, most of the time at the University of Oklahoma as Research Professor and Director of the Courses in Professional Writing. During World War I he served as a captain in the Field Artillery. He is the author of twenty-four books, mostly about the Old West, the Plains Indians, and the cow towns.

WE WERE THERE BOOKS

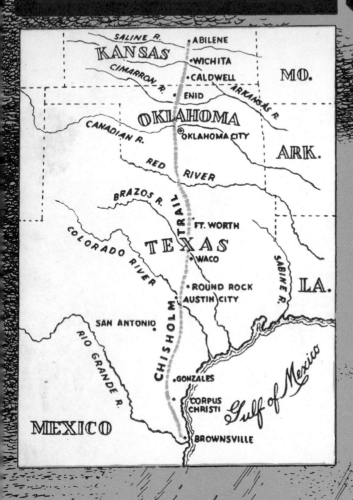

SALINE R.

KANSAS
• ABILENE
• WICHITA
• CALDWELL
• ENID

CIMARRON R.

MO.

ARKANSAS R.

OKLAHOMA
CANADIAN R.
⊙ OKLAHOMA CITY

ARK.

RED RIVER

BRAZOS R.

TEXAS
FT. WORTH
• WACO
• ROUND ROCK
AUSTIN CITY

COLORADO RIVER

SABINE R.

LA.

SAN ANTONIO

RIO GRANDE R.

CHISHOLM TRAIL

• GONZALES
• CORPUS CHRISTI

Gulf of Mexico

MEXICO

• BROWNSVILLE